"I laughed so hard I cried on multiple occasions while reading
MARSHMALLOW S'MORE MURDER! Girl Scouts, the CIA,
and the Yakuza... what could possibly go wrong?"
—*Fresh Fiction*

"Darkly funny and wildly over the top, this mystery answers the
burning question, 'Do assassin skills and Girl Scout merit badges
mix...' one truly original and wacky novel!"
—*RT BOOK REVIEWS*

"Those who like dark humor will enjoy a look into the deadliest
female assassin and PTA mom's life."
—*Parkersburg News*

"Mixing a deadly sense of humor and plenty of sexy sizzle,
Leslie Langtry creates a brilliantly original, laughter-rich mix of
contemporary romance and suspense in *'Scuse Me While I Kill
This Guy.*"
—*Chicago Tribune*

"The beleaguered soccer mom assassin concept is a winner, and
Langtry gets the fun started from page one with a myriad of
clever details."
—*Publisher's Weekly*

BOOKS BY LESLIE LANGTRY

Merry Wrath Mysteries:
Merit Badge Murder
Mint Cookie Murder
Scout Camp Murder
(short story in the Killer Beach Reads collection)
Marshmallow S'More Murder
Movie Night Murder
Mud Run Murder
Fishing Badge Murder
(short story in the Pushing Up Daisies collection)
Motto for Murder
Map Skills Murder
Mean Girl Murder
Marriage Vow Murder
Mystery Night Murder
Meerkats and Murder
Make Believe Murder

Greatest Hits Mysteries:
'Scuse Me While I Kill This Guy
Guns Will Keep Us Together
Stand By Your Hitman
I Shot You Babe
Paradise By The Rifle Sights
Snuff the Magic Dragon
My Heroes Have Always Been Hitmen
Have Yourself a Deadly Little Christmas (a holiday short story)
Four Killing Birds (a holiday short story)

Aloha Lagoon Mysteries:
Ukulele Murder
Ukulele Deadly

Other Works:
Sex, Lies, & Family Vacations

MAKE BELIEVE MURDER

A Merry Wrath Mystery

USA TODAY BESTSELLING AUTHOR
Leslie Langtry

MAKE
BELIEVE
MURDER

CHAPTER ONE

———

"All rise!" a voice cried out. I couldn't tell if it was male or female, but it was definitely a teenager and I'd *definitely* heard it before.

As for the request to rise, well that would be a bit tricky, considering that I was tied to a chair with a hood over my head. Rough rope cut into my wrists and ankles. Too bad it wasn't zip ties. I was good at getting out of those.

A burst of cicadas screeched around me from every direction, telling me I was outside and it was most likely evening. The hood was open a bit at the bottom, and I could see weeds and dirt. That could be the backyard at my old house. I wasn't much of a gardener. In fact, I was a little embarrassed that whoever had taken me could see that.

The last thing I remembered was taking a nap in my hammock at my house. And by *house*, I meant the one I shared with my husband, not the house across the street that I still owned, to the complete consternation of said husband.

Where was I, and why was I tied up? Had I been captured by the Russians? Hmmm…no, not if this was rope that held me down. Like me, they preferred zip ties. The Russians went berserk when that particular form of bondage was invented. Like it was Christmas in Moscow and Russian Santa was actually sober. Spies over there used them on everything from Ukrainians to leftover salads.

You might think, hey! The voices I heard spoke English! They must be Americans. And in most cases you'd be right. But once I'd been kidnapped by an Estonian arms dealer who was a bit obsessed with America and wanted to show off his newly acquired Bronx accent. He also only ate hot dogs and Velveeta cheese.

So, you see, it wouldn't do to guess until I knew more.

My name is Merry Wrath, and for several years, I was a spy with the CIA, until the vice president "accidentally" outed me to get back at my senator dad. Originally, my name was Fionnaghuala (pronounced "Finella") Merrygold Czrygy, but I changed it to Merry Wrath and moved back to my hometown of Who's There, Iowa to help run a Girl Scout troop.

Makes perfect sense, right?

There was a tapping sound, kind of like a baseball bat on a rock.

"I command the Dark Forces to accept this old lady as our tribute," a male voice squeaked, "so that we may have superpowers!"

Old lady? That's it. I put some effort into it, and in a split second the ropes binding my wrists fell off easily, and then I untied my legs and pulled off my hood.

"Stewie!" I shouted sternly as I got to my feet.

The short, fat kid with wiry red hair was dressed in a dark, wizardy robe with a cow skull perched on top of his head that only helped to give him three more inches, bringing him up to the robust height of 5'4". I'd met the kid only a month or so ago when I walked in on him and a kid named Robby engaging in some cosplay at the zoo.

"You're not supposed to do that!" Stewie stamped his foot, and the cow skull fell to the ground, landing with a very un-wizardy *thunk*.

I stalked toward him. "Why was I tied to that chair?"

The other teen druids looked around anxiously, like they were about to get grounded from their video games.

Stewie knew he was losing them. Raising his arms dramatically over his head, which wasn't easy since he was so rotund, he screamed, "We are the Cult of NicoDerm!" His fingers wiggled at me, reminding me of jazz hands. "*Fear us!*"

"NicoDerm...like the nicotine patch?" I asked as I placed my hands on my hips.

"What?" Stewie's face fell. "No!" he shouted. "We are *Dread Incarnate!*"

I shook my head. "Not unless you mean to inspire fear in those who try to quit smoking."

His arms came down, and he scooped up the cow skull. His hair had matted against his skull in a way that looked like he had horns on either side of his head. I had no idea if that was intentional.

"Who is this chick?" A tall, skinny girl with stringy brown hair stepped forward. "I thought you were getting us a proper sacrifice."

I narrowed my eyes. "You were going to sacrifice me?"

"Not really," a tall boy on my left with a serious acne affliction said in an unnaturally low voice. "We weren't going to kill you or nothing. We were just going to draw a little blood with this knife." He held up a certified Boy Scout pocketknife with the Phillips-head screwdriver sticking out.

"Oh, that makes me feel so much better." I shook my head.

Stewie shrieked, "*I am Odious, the Demigod!*"

I looked down at the chair. "Is this from my house?"

"I knew you couldn't pull it off," the girl sneered. "You really are a Stewbutt."

"You should've gotten us a virgin." Another girl in back pointed at me. "When they're old like that, they're not virgins anymore."

"I've heard that." The boy with the low voice nodded. "It falls off them or something when they hit menopause at thirty."

"First off"—I glared at the kids—"I'm not old. I'm not even thirty. And secondly, I don't think you understand how virginity works, but I'm not the one who's going to explain it to you."

"Who *is* this woman?" the squeaky boy asked.

Stewie seemed to shrink. "Some crazy lady who talks to birds."

Every fake druid turned towards me, staring at me.

"She can talk to birds!" The girl bowed down to me.

"She's magical!" The squeaky boy did the same.

* * *

"And," I explained, "that's how I became the Bird Lady Protector of the Cult of NicoDerm."

Rex's right eyebrow went up. To be honest, I'm surprised he let me go on this long. He didn't seem amused ten minutes ago when I walked through the front door with leaves in my hair, carrying one of our dining room chairs. I forgot to ask Stewie how he got it but had no intention of going back to ask because they were in the process of collecting bird feathers to make me a crown, most likely woven with a healthy dose of surly despair.

"That's your excuse for being late for dinner?" The corner of his mouth twitched a bit. "How did they kidnap you, and how did they get a dining room chair?"

"Remember when Bart house-sat for us last weekend so we could go to Chicago?"

Rex nodded. "Yes. How does Bart figure into this?"

Bart was Betty's older brother. Betty was one of my more precocious Scouts.

"Bart found the chloroform wipes, took one, and sold it to Stewie for fifty bucks. Stewie and some kid with bad skin then used it on me while I was napping in the yard. They grabbed the chair at that time."

"He confessed all of that?" My husband's right eyebrow went up.

"Well," I admitted, "after I stood on his neck and threatened to do terrible things to his more sensitive body parts with a sharpened pinecone."

"Damn," Rex mused as he looked at our pets (which included a Scottish deerhound, a narcoleptic cat who looked like Elvis, and an obese older cat who looked like Hitler). "I really liked Bart. Now we'll need another house sitter."

Philby the Hitler cat meowed loudly as if to say we didn't need a house sitter since she could handle things on her own. Leonard, the dog, whimpered in dissent because one of Philby's favorite pastimes was tormenting him. Martini had no opinion because, yet again, she was asleep, this time facedown and spread-eagle on my foot.

I pulled the pinecone, its scales sharpened into spikes, from my back pocket. "I can have a little talk with Bart too, if you'd like."

He shook his head. "No time right now. You'd better get ready."

My husband, the town's only detective, was dressed in a suit. We were supposed to have dinner with Dr. Soo Jin Body, the county medical examiner, and her new boyfriend and Iowa State Trooper, Eduardo Ruiz. I'd been looking forward all week to meeting and interrogating him.

"Give me ten minutes!" I shouted over my shoulder as I raced up the stairs.

Seven minutes later, I was showered and dressed in a simple blue dress and black ballet flats. My short, curly hair was still a bit damp, but I thought that was okay because now I had a killer dinner story.

* * *

"You made it!" Soo Jin jumped up from her chair when we entered Trattoria Italiano, the nicest restaurant in town. The drop-dead gorgeous woman threw her arms around me and crushed me in a hug.

I squeezed back. "Sorry! I had to disrupt a teenage druid sacrifice." I turned to her date, an equally gorgeous man with dark wavy hair and a warm, crooked grin that could melt pavement. "You must be Eduardo."

The man smiled and planted a kiss on each cheek. "Eddie, please."

We sat down, and Soo Jin poured us a glass of wine. "Now, what's this about some druid sacrifice?"

"They weren't going to sacrifice a druid," I explained. "*I* was the sacrifice." I retold the story, adding a few new flourishes, like a newt and crystal ball. At one point I had a bald eagle swoop in and land on my shoulder.

Rex wisely said nothing. And I loved him for that.

Eddie looked at me curiously when I finished.

Soo Jin put her hand on his arm. "This kind of thing happens to her all the time."

She was right. It did. Well, not the sacrifice part. That was fairly new.

"What are you going to do with those kids?" Eddie asked. All I knew about him was that he was a state trooper and Soo Jin really, really, really liked him. She'd actually said it three times.

Rex sighed. "Not much. I'll just drag them in for questioning on how they managed to steal a chair from our house."

Eddie looked at me. "But they kidnapped your wife…"

I waved him off. "It happens more often than you'd think."

"And trust me," Rex said as he took my hand in his, "Merry can take care of herself."

The man looked positively confused. Soo Jin whispered in his ear, and he smiled. She probably told him she'd explain later.

We ordered, and I decided to put the whole druid thing behind us. "Eddie, I'm so glad we're finally getting to meet you."

Rex smiled warmly. "It's nice to have another man at the table. Usually I'm surrounded by Merry and a cloud of little girls."

"Oh right." Eddie relaxed, leaning back in his chair. "The Girl Scout troop. I've heard a lot about them."

Of course he had. It was probably the first thing Soo Jin told him. My troop was legendary. My girls could solve murders, take down bad guys with a lollipop stick, and come up with diabolical plans that would make the mafia weep. I told him a couple of stories of the troop's exploits in Washington DC during a mud run fundraiser at camp and recently at a murder mystery night gone wrong.

"Wow," Eddie gasped when I finished. "It's nice to see such strong, independent girls."

I liked him already. But now, the nicey-nice was over because it was time to interrogate him to find out if he was good enough for my friend. So far he had a very high rating, but that could change. And Soo Jin, crushing on him with her three *really*s, might not be a good judge of character. After all, the woman worked almost exclusively with dead people.

"Eddie, tell me about yourself," I demanded.

He actually blushed. The man actually blushed. "I grew up in Chicago," he started. "Went to Northwestern and got into law enforcement. It's a boring story."

"I'm sure it isn't." I smiled. "Tell me everything about your life."

"Merry," Rex warned, squeezing my hand hard. "We're not here to interrogate the man."

I ignored him. "Eddie, your comment about the girls means you obviously have feminist leanings, which is good. But how do you feel about women in the CIA?"

Rex rolled his eyes. "Eddie, you don't have to answer that."

Soo Jin giggled adorably.

"It's okay." Eddie waved my husband off. "Soo Jin told me about your past. I think it's amazing, all the things you've been able to do. I hope if I have a little girl someday that she's in your troop."

I blushed in spite of myself. It was an impulse I could usually control, mainly because nobody flattered me like this.

"Merry's solved a few murders around here, too," Soo Jin said. "She's very smart."

This time my already red face caught fire.

Eddie took a drink from his glass of wine. "Sheriff Carnack has told me a little about that. My only concern is in hoping others don't try to do the same and step on the toes of local law enforcement."

What?

Rex laughed. "Eddie, you've passed my test with flying colors. Dinner's on me."

"Well, sure," I stumbled. "I don't think people should take the law into their own hands. I just happen to have experiences in my past that give me an edge."

Eddie held his hands up. "I'm so sorry, Merry. I didn't mean to imply that you were acting above the law."

"No, please, by all means," Rex said. "Imply it. She won't listen anyway."

Soo Jin protested, "She's actually been very helpful on a number of cases."

Now that someone had come to my rescue, I decided to let up on Eddie. Rex, on the other hand, would hear about this later.

"It's okay. I shouldn't have come here planning to interrogate you. If Soo Jin likes you, then that's good enough for me."

That didn't mean I was done questioning him.

By the time the food came, I'd learned most of what I needed to know. The important things, like how he treated my friend and what his opinion was on cats that looked like Hitler. By the way, Eddie said he'd never hold a cat's appearance against her.

By dessert we were all laughing like old friends. Eddie was nice and a calm, quiet man. He seemed the perfect complement to the bubbly Soo Jin. Kind of like how Rex was a grownup who ate healthy, balanced meals, while I still ate Pizza Rolls and believed sugar was at the top of the food pyramid. That kind of thing.

Eddie passed my test, and I officially liked him. As we breezed through dinner and dessert, I relaxed. A little. There'd have to be a few more conversations and a late-night background check I'd get from hacking into the CIA's database, but for now, Eddie Ruiz was alright by me.

As the night wrapped up and we walked to our cars, I spotted someone lurking by the dumpster. It was tough to tell, but it looked like a woman. I couldn't see her face, but her stance was unusual, and I'd seen it before. And she was staring at me.

No way. It can't be!

I grabbed an old fast food bag from the floor of my minivan. "I'm gonna toss this real quick," I said to Rex.

"Good idea," my very neat and tidy husband agreed. "But why not take more stuff…" His voice trailed off because I was already halfway there.

The woman slipped out of sight as I reached the dumpster. I tossed the bag and looked around. A giggle came from the shadows of the building on my left. A very unusual giggle.

It couldn't possibly be who I thought it was.

"Hilly?" I hissed into the darkness. "Is that you?"

A woman with long brown hair in a braid down her back and a very athletic build stepped out to meet me.

"You remember me!" She threw her arms around my neck and jumped up and down, her shoulder repeatedly smashing into my chin.

I pulled away and stared. "Hilly! What are you doing here?"

This wasn't just any blast from the past. Hilly was an assassin with the CIA (an agency that doesn't have assassins—I'm required to say that). Her appearance anywhere wasn't necessarily good. It usually meant that someone was about to die.

Hopefully, it wasn't me.

CHAPTER TWO

———

"Are you working, Hilly?" I asked my old colleague. *And is it me you're here for?* I didn't ask out loud.

She rolled her eyes. "No, duh! I'm on vacation. I came here to see you!"

I looked around. "In a dark alley, by a dumpster, at night?"

She cocked her head to one side. "Too weird?"

Actually, it wasn't weird at all…for her. Hilly's favorite method of disposal was always dropping the deceased into a dumpster. Always. Well, except for this one time in Singapore when she had to schlep the body to Malaysia to dispose of it. Singapore is not big on public garbage. Hilly was just being polite.

I glanced into the dumpster, just in case. It was hard to tell because it was dark and full of garbage bags, any one of which could hold body parts. But maybe I was just being paranoid. Then again…

"Seriously," I repeated. "What are you doing here?"

She shrugged. "Seriously. I haven't used any vacation days in, like, ever. Human Resources was throwing around terms like 'before she's too far gone,' and 'apocalyptic psychological damage.' So, I decided to come and visit you."

I remembered how hard I'd been on Eddie earlier in the evening and forced myself to relax. In spite of her being *Killy Hilly*, I really liked her.

"Where are you staying?" I asked. There were only a couple of hotels in town, which ranged from Radisson to This-is-Where-You-Die (a somewhat sketchy motel just outside of town).

She paused, looking perplexed. "I just got here. I saw you and thought I'd surprise you!"

That's when I noticed the usual black SUV favored by spies, Feds, and Albanian figure skaters parked behind the dumpster.

"You can stay with us tonight." I took her arm. "Come on. You can meet my husband, Rex."

My easygoing husband was more than gracious once I told him about my colleague (I might've left out what she did for the CIA), and she followed us on the five-minute trip to our house. Everything in Who's There was five minutes away—the town council was considering that for a new community slogan to replace the somewhat creepy: *Come for a visit and stay forever!*

Hilly Vinton walked through the front door with one suitcase. She paused in the doorway and looked around carefully. Force of habit from a lifetime of being paranoid. Once we enticed her over the threshold, she *oohed* and *ahhed* about the place.

I had to give Rex all the credit for décor. It was something I wasn't good at. At my other house, my first foray into decorating was to turn Dora the Explorer bedsheets into living room drapes. I had those for a year before Kelly (my best friend and co-leader) made me take them down.

Philby ignored us, like she usually did. She was in the front window, staring at my house, tail twitching. She'd been doing this a lot lately. Last year we'd found live mice in Rex's house, so whenever she was at my house, she was in the window, staring at this place. I wondered for only a moment if I now had mice at my house. Either that or the cat was insane—and both were very plausible explanations.

Sitting in the living room, Hilly folded her legs under her and was the subject of interest by two cats (Philby had deemed her worthy of giving up surveillance) and one Scottish deerhound. She ruffled Leonard's fur but looked curiously at the two cats.

"Merry," she said. "Did you know one of your cats—"

"Looks like Hitler?" I nodded. "Yeah. Once you get to know her, you'll find out it suits her because she really is a dictator."

She shook her head. "No. I was going to say that one of your cats looks like Elvis."

She was talking about Martini—Philby the feline fuhrer's daughter who bore a resemblance to the King and who's main hobby was narcolepsy. The small cat climbed up into the assassin's lap and fell asleep in seconds, legs akimbo.

The animals seemed to like Hilly with one exception. Philby sat on the coffee table, glaring at our guest. A judgy animal on her best day, the fat cat usually didn't gel with folks immediately.

"So," Rex said with a smile. "Can I get anyone a glass of wine or a beer?"

I raised my hand, but Hilly cocked her head to one side again. "I'd prefer Ouzo. Do you have that?"

My husband shook his head. "Sorry. I can get a bottle tomorrow, though."

"Okay," my friend said. "How about a cup of coffee instead?"

Rex nodded and left for the kitchen.

"How long do you think you'll stay?" I asked.

She frowned, her gray eyes wrinkling in the corners. "I don't know. How long does one normally vacation for?"

I shrugged. "I'm not sure. A week, maybe?" I hadn't had a lot of experience with vacations, unless you counted camping trips with my troop. And even then, a week felt like a month, so maybe I wasn't the right person to ask.

She brightened. "A week it is, then! I'll check into a hotel tomorrow."

Rex appeared with her coffee, only to have Hilly ask where the guest room was. We led her upstairs, and she said good night, closing the door behind her.

"That was, um, unusual," Rex said a few minutes later as we got ready for bed.

"Yeah, Hilly marches to the beat of a different saxophone."

"Drummer," he corrected as he slid between the sheets.

I shook my head. "No, saxophone. She was, at one time, a concert musician."

My husband laughed. I loved making him laugh. But I wasn't kidding about the saxophone. She literally played Carnegie Hall. Twice.

"You worked with her?" he asked.

"Um, yes?"

"Merry?" He gave me that arch look that said he knew I was holding something back.

I blew out a breath. "She's an assassin for the CIA."

He frowned. "I thought the CIA doesn't assassinate people?"

I shook my head. "We don't. And we don't have assassins. That would be illegal."

"But you just said she…"

"Ah. I can see how that might seem confusing. Hilly isn't an assassin," I corrected. "But she really is."

My husband looked at me for a moment. "You certainly cleared that up. I'm not so sure having a killer under our roof is such a good idea."

I rolled my eyes. "She's an *assassin*, not a killer. It's her job. And it's only for one night, I promise."

"An assassin is a killer," Rex corrected.

I shook my head. "The CIA doesn't have assassins. I keep having to tell you that. Think of her as a problem solver. Does that help?"

He reached for the lamp. "As long as we are not the problem she has to solve." Rex turned off the light. "And just for tonight, right?"

"Right!" I agreed.

While my husband slept beside me, I thought about Hilly. She was a friend. Even saved my life once. And it would be fun to hang out with a colleague who was someone other than Riley, my former handler who'd set up shop as a private investigator here in town.

Hilly and I could talk shop. I couldn't do that with very many people. And I decided I wasn't going to put her in a hotel. She could stay at my house across the street. With that decision made, I drifted off to sleep.

* * *

Rex had to leave for work first thing in the morning, and Hilly didn't come down until after he'd left.

"I like your pajamas," I said.

She smiled. "I like yours."

Turned out we were both wearing Dora the Explorer jammies.

"I think secretly," Hilly said in a stage whisper, "Dora is a spy. That monkey, Boots, is her handler."

My head kind of exploded. I'd always had the same thought, thus leading to the bedsheet curtains. Kelly was right about making me take them down and replace them with something boring. In espionage, you had to blend in, be invisible. Which was hard to do with such awesome drapes.

"I think you should stay at my house instead of a hotel," I said in a rush of words as I pulled back the curtain and pointed at the little ranch house directly across from us. "It's fully furnished, so you should be comfortable there."

"I love it!" Hilly clapped her hands at my offer. "I'll be just across the street, and we can do stuff together!" Then she cocked her head to one side. "What are you supposed to do on vacation?"

"Well…you see the sights, I think." I tried to think of what those sights in Who's There were. "We have an awesome zoo. And we can go to Des Moines."

There wasn't much else unless I took her to all the places where people had died around me…or because of me. That might fill up a week. Then again, wasn't vacation where you did stuff *other* than work? I'd have to rethink that.

Hilly looked serious. "Do they have any red wolves? I'm kind of afraid of red wolves."

I stared at her. "I've seen you take on five giant men, armed only with a pumice stone and a Slip 'N Slide! How is it you are afraid of wolves, red ones in particular?"

She shrugged. "I don't know. I just woke up one day and thought *red wolves are scary*!"

"Well." I buttered some toast. "You're in for a treat, because I just happen to be friends with a red wolf, and I'll introduce you two."

If that seemed like a strange statement, she didn't say so.

As we ate, the animals stared at our food. Philby was drooling at the other end of the table because of the heaping plate of bacon I'd made. I wasn't much of a cook but had recently added bacon to my repertoire. And to celebrate, we now ate it every day. Eggs were next on the agenda, and someday I might go so far as to attempt waffles, but it was probably a good idea for me to take things slow.

We got dressed, and I took her over to my house. The animals were sad because I didn't take them with me, something I did a lot. Philby would rotate between stalking the basement for mice that weren't there and staring at the other house like she wanted to be there instead. Martini would fall asleep on top of the fridge or, in one scary incident, inside the oven. Leonard liked sleeping on my bed since Rex didn't allow that at our house.

"I like this place!" Hilly said as she walked into the living room.

My little ranch house was perfect, and I was having a hard time parting with it, something that perplexed my husband. I showed her around and insisted she take the guest room, a room that was ten times better than my room. A few years back, I kind of shot up the place. Kelly took me shopping for all new furniture, and now, compared to my IKEA bedroom, I thought of the guest room as the palace at Versailles.

She put her suitcase on the bed and began to unpack. It was weird to see my friend do that. Assassins have to pack quickly and travel light. Suitcases couldn't keep up with the stresses of the job because it's almost impossible to run away from a Chechen with an Uzi while dragging a rolling case. I say "almost" because on one occasion, the man from Chechnya was also hauling a suitcase and his Uzi jammed.

Or if you had back-to-back assignments, like Hilly did once when she had to take out a target on the southernmost tip of Argentina on a Friday morning, one in Northern Finland at lunchtime, and then end the day with a clean kill in Qatar. The wheels literally fell off her carry-on at the end of that day. And if you think it's easy finding a quality replacement suitcase in Qatar, you'd be wrong.

I've always suspected that the CIA's travel department was made up of sadists. After all, three of them were dominatrices (I knew this because two wore their leathers to work and the other always carried a riding crop and insisted you call her *My Overlord*) and one was an out-of-the-closet psychopath named Orville who collected human teeth (the good news was you could get an upgrade to first class if you brought him two molars or a canine.

"Rex seems nice," Hilly said as she took her shampoo to the bathroom. "And marrying a cop is a great cover."

"Rex isn't cover. He's legitimately my husband."

She stared at me. "Wow. You, like, *love* him and everything?"

I nodded. "I do."

Hilly sat on the edge of the bed. "I don't think I'll ever get married. I don't have a very good opinion of men."

I tossed a pillow at her. "That's because the only men you have ever known have been targets or have tried to kill you."

She returned the throw with such speed and gusto that the pillow knocked me to the floor. "I've never really looked at it that way." Hilly cocked her head to one side. She was starting to resemble a cockatoo. "Maybe I'll meet someone here…on my vacation."

The men I knew in Who's There shared a police lineup in my mind, making it tough to find the right candidate. After ruling out a couple of farmers who liked animals more than people, my nice but shy dentist who whispered everything, and a few guys I went to high school with for whom the mullet should be declared the state haircut, I came up empty.

"But you still work in Virginia," I said. "Having a boyfriend here would be tough."

"Yeah, but I'm almost never at Langley." She jumped to her feet. "Oh well. It was a nice idea while it lasted."

I laughed. "You're so decisive."

"In my line of work, I have to be." Hilly put her hands on her hips. "Sometimes you only have a split second to act when things go wrong."

I knew she was right. Riley had told me stories he'd heard about her. Hilly was great at snap decisions. One time her target appeared right there in the open, on a busy street in Kenya. She had only a moment to hit the gas and run him down. Twice.

"This is going to be fun!" I said.

My cell went off. It was Riley texting to ask me to stop by. I said my good-byes, gave her a key, and told her to go ahead and settle in.

*   *   *

"What's up?" I asked as I walked into the little office in the strip mall. "Hey, Claire," I said to the knockout blonde receptionist, who responded with a silent nod. It was the most conversation I'd gotten out of her in weeks.

Riley Andrews, my former handler, had retired early and set up shop in Who's There, Iowa, to be a private investigator. He was always trying to get me to come and work for him. Was that why he'd called me? If it was, he'd better be prepared for disappointment. Few women ever said *no* to the handsome ex-spy with the perpetually golden skin, wavy blond surfer hair, and dazzlingly white teeth. Which was why I always relished the opportunity to do so.

Riley didn't look up from his computer monitor. "Over here," he said.

I joined him. The man and I had been partners for almost a decade, and we'd even dated for like, a minute. Riley was a true lady-killer…in pretty much every sense of the word. Well, not since he'd gone legit. I mean, if he was seducing and killing women in the middle of Iowa, I'd hear about it.

"I found something," he said as I walked over and stood behind him.

"Is this from here?" A grainy black and white screen outside Marlowe's, one of the two grocery stores in town, showed the back of a woman with long, light-colored hair. "Lana?" I gasped. "She's here! I knew it!"

A long time ago I'd turned Lana, a Russian spy, to our side. Years later, she tried to kill me. And more recently she'd escaped from a high-security penitentiary. I was the only one who believed she was in Iowa, and in the last six months, I'd had some strange pseudo run-ins with her.

"I think so," Riley said. "It's hard to tell, but look at what she's carrying."

I leaned in. "That's what makes you think she's here? Because she's carrying a purse?"

Riley shook his head. "Not that. Look at her other hand."

I leaned in closer. "Oh, wow. Yeah, that's her alright."

In Lana's hand was a large photo of me. It wasn't very good. I'd been at a Girl Scout rally and had a little too much cotton candy, resulting in a huge disturbing smile and wide eyes. It was not my favorite photo, but the girls in my troop had put up 11x17" copies all over town a few months ago. I thought I'd taken them down, but apparently I'd missed one.

This was good news—proof of what I'd suspected for a long time. Lana was lurking around Who's There, and this proved that I hadn't been imagining things every time I thought I'd seen her. To be honest, even though Lana probably wanted to kill me, it was a relief seeing her in the image.

"Come on!" I shouted. "Let's go nail her!"

But Riley didn't get up. "Wrath, that footage is from yesterday."

I slumped into a chair. "At least she's here." I brightened. "And guess who else is here? Someone who can help!"

Riley's brows furrowed. "Who?"

"Hilly!"

His jaw dropped, and he looked around nervously. "Hilly Vinton? Is *here*?"

Oh right. Riley didn't like her. How could I have forgotten that?

"She's taking her first vacation ever," I added. "And she decided to visit me!"

Riley shook his head slowly. "And you don't find that suspicious? Come on, Merry! You know better than that!"

"Hilly saved my life once, are you forgetting?"

He threw his arms into the air. "From a car bomb that *she* set!"

I rolled my eyes. "That was never proven."

"Has it occurred to you," Riley asked, "that she might be here to do a job?"

"You have never liked her, Riley. I don't know why I'm even listening to you."

Of all the women in the CIA, Hilly was the only one who didn't fall for my former handler's charms…present company included. It always bugged him that she wasn't interested.

"Hilly Vinton never took one day off. Not one, in all of her years with the Agency," he pressed, ignoring my comment. "So why take one now?"

"Look." I pointed at him. "She's a friend, and she came to visit. You can't go through your life not trusting people."

He nodded vigorously. "You can when that friend is more lethal than anthrax."

Claire looked up from her computer as if interested in this conversation.

Riley pulled me back a few feet and lowered his voice. "Don't you think it's also coincidental that Hilly's here and now we have a legit Lana sighting?"

I shrugged him off. "Maybe. But I've been telling you that Lana's here for months now, and you've never believed it."

"She could be here to kill Lana," he said.

I thought about that for a second. If it was true, yay! And it made me sad to think she wasn't here to hang out with me.

"That would imply that the CIA knows Lana is here," I said. "And that proves I've been right all this time!"

Riley interrupted my victory dance, which included the Electric Boogaloo, the Chicken Dance, and something called the Bangladesh Sweatshop Polka.

"If Lana is here, she's here for one reason—to kill you."

I couldn't argue with that. It had been on my mind ever since she'd escaped from prison and was seen here. "She'll have to come into the open to do that. And I'll be ready for her."

Riley was known to go off the rails every rare now and then, but it was unusual. It was nice to know he cared. And

Svetlana Babikova was an extremely dangerous spy who hated me.

"So," I said. "What are we going to do about her?"

He sighed. "Give me a day or two to pull some strings and see what I can find out. And I also want to know why Hilly is here. I'll let you know what I find out."

"Fine, you do what you think you need to." I headed for the door. "Bye, Claire."

The gorgeous secretary didn't even look up.

As I drove back to my old house, I thought about what Riley had said. He was wrong, of course, about the car bomb. Hilly had been tailing an arms dealer in Colombia at the same time I'd been undercover with Carlos the Armadillo. One day, as I'd just climbed into my car, this brunette amazon I'd never seen before came racing up to me, tore open the door, threw me out of the car, and dragged me away. The vehicle exploded a few seconds later.

Hilly had given me the secret handshake, and I'd responded with the correlating passwords, which confirmed we were playing for the same team. We've been friends ever since. The spy had told me she'd seen me before at Langley. She'd said the guy she had been tailing had mistaken my car for another and set the bomb. Hilly had waited to see what would happen, but when she spotted me, she changed her mind.

Hilly did get that guy. Killed him with a book to the throat and threw him in a dumpster. The police didn't even investigate. Apparently that kind of thing is very common down there.

While she was here, I should have her show my Girl Scout troop a couple of techniques. Especially Betty. She'd love the book thing. I wasn't sure Betty read, but she might start if she thought she could wield it as a weapon, which seemed like a win.

I pulled into my old driveway and shut off the car. Hilly's SUV was still parked there.

I wasn't worried about her. She was just here to see what a normal life was like. Considering that she grew up in Toledo, that was completely understandable.

It was a nice, bright sunny day, and the temperature was fairly mild for June. The girls were out of school, and we had a meeting coming up. It would be the perfect time to introduce Hilly. Like a sort of career day…with an assassin (who is, of course, *not* an assassin). I wished they'd had that when I was a kid. How cool would it have been to learn about picking locks with a bobby pin or making bombs out of Pixy Stix and Kool-Aid?

After inserting the key into the lock, I reminded myself that I had a guest who probably wanted some modicum of privacy, so I knocked. There was no answer. Was she sleeping? In the shower? I knocked again and called out her name, but again, there was no response.

Very quietly I let myself into the house. She wasn't in the living room or kitchen, and the shower wasn't running. As I walked down the hallway, I kept away from the creakier floorboards. If she was asleep, I didn't want to wake her.

The door to the guest room was slightly open, and I could see her curled up in bed, out cold. Huh. She'd just slept through the night. Then again, this was her vacation. Maybe that's what assassins did on their time off. Taking out targets can be exhausting.

Very carefully, I shut her door and walked back through the house. I was just checking the fridge to see if I needed to make a grocery run for my guest, when through the kitchen window I spotted something in the backyard.

It looked like a body. The dead kind.

Dammit.

CHAPTER THREE

———

Moments later, I was kneeling in the grass over the body of a woman who was maybe in her midthirties. Even with her staring glassily at the sky, I still checked for a pulse and then breathing. She wasn't doing either.

Who was this, and why was she in my yard? Before dialing Rex, I took a couple of photos on my phone. Then I phoned my husband what was up and pulled up a lawn chair to wait.

I knew better than to check for a wallet. Rex wouldn't be happy if my prints were found on it. And since the medical examiner was the only one who could touch the body first, I'd be breaking the rules. So, I studied the dead woman and the area surrounding her.

She was shorter than me. Maybe about 5'6" to my 5'9". Blue eyes, red hair, and freckles, she could be anyone. She was dressed casually in shorts, tennis shoes, and a T-shirt, as if she'd just been taking a walk to my backyard to die. There was no visible injury, so I had no idea what killed her.

I didn't recognize her from the neighborhood. And no, I don't know my neighbors. But old habits die hard, and I've spent some time watching people go by. I knew what houses they came out of and at what time. I knew what their cars looked like and which routes they took for work. Not that I followed them or anything (I'm not a total basket case). I put secret hidden cameras up on all the light posts. Much more efficient. Too bad I didn't have any on my alley or aimed at my hedge-hidden backyard. I'd have to fix that. Would've blown this case right open.

Rex walked through the bushes that surrounded my yard, followed by Officer Kevin Dooley, a mouth-breathing

Neanderthal I went to school with. Kevin had a clear plastic container with a large piece of cake he was eating with a fork. Frankly, I'd have been worried if he hadn't turned up with food. This guy was always eating on the job. The day he doesn't have his whole arm in a bag of fried pork rinds or isn't covered in powdered sugar from donuts will be the day the apocalypse begins.

My husband knelt down beside the woman as Soo Jin burst through the bushes.

"You'll be amazed to hear," he said, "that this actually comes as a shock."

My jaw dropped. "Since when are you surprised by a body in my presence?"

He didn't look at me as he studied the victim's hands without touching them. Since Soo Jin had first rights to the body. Rex had to wait until she was finished before he could examine the corpse.

"I kind of hoped this was all behind us," Rex sighed.

Soo Jin spoke up. "I can't find any sign of a wound in front. I'll need to take her back to the morgue."

"Could it have been some sort of accident?" I ventured.

She shrugged just as two men I knew vaguely as her assistants came through the bushes with a stretcher on wheels.

Rex and I said nothing as the woman was taken away.

"Is Hilly here?" Rex asked. "I noticed her SUV in the driveway."

I nodded. "She's napping. We should probably go ask her if she knows anything."

"Do you think she might have killed the victim?" Rex asked.

"What?" I jumped. "No! Why would she kill some random civilian on her first day of vacation? Who does that?"

Rex held his hands up. "Don't get defensive. I'm just doing my job. She is, after all, an assassin for the CIA…"

I shook my head. "The CIA doesn't have assassins."

"Why do you keep saying that when it's clearly not the case?"

"I had to sign an agreement to make that claim every time the words *CIA* and *assassin* were used in the same sentence. It's standard protocol."

Rex's right eyebrow went up. "So, you're saying she really is an assassin for the CIA, but you can't say out loud that she is?"

I nodded. "She's absolutely not an assassin."

Back in the guest room, I quietly searched the two nightstands and under the pillows without waking my guest. Have you ever woken a sleeping assassin? I don't recommend it. With these professionals, their training kicks in before their eyes open. Rufus, another CIA assassin (we don't have assassins) had overslept, and Riley and I needed to get him on an airplane. He'd choked me for thirty seconds until his eyes flew open. I've never heard someone apologize so much in my whole career.

"Why did you search the nightstand and pillows?" Rex whispered.

"Weapons. These people usually have something close to grab in a pinch. I once knew a Colombian hitwoman who slept with a flamethrower."

He folded his arms. "You're joking."

I shook my head. "In hindsight, it was a bad decision on her part. She tripped the trigger in her sleep one night and singed off her eyebrows and hair and totally destroyed her 18th Century four-post bed. Her eyebrows never did grow back."

From a safe distance, standing in front of Rex, I started calling her name, softly at first and then louder.

The woman quickly reached down to her sock and pulled a razor on me while getting to her feet. Once her eyes opened, she dropped the weapon and smiled.

"Oh. Hi, Merry."

"Sorry to wake you up," I started.

Rex cleared his throat. "Hilly, I have a couple of questions, if you don't mind."

This, I was learning, was detective talk. Rex never gave anything away until he'd asked a bunch of questions. It was kind of annoying, really, but I did love watching him work.

She looked from me to him. "There's a body, isn't there? I didn't do it."

"How did you know there's a body?" I asked, ruining Rex's timing.

Hilly stretched. "I've only ever been woken up by a person other than my mother twice. Both times, it was because there was a body."

She began jogging in place then followed with deep lunges.

"By a person?" Rex asked.

I nodded. "Hilly uses her cell for an alarm."

"The first time was in Switzerland," she said without panting, which impressed me. "I was in the wrong place at the wrong time when this skier was found shot to death outside the door of my hotel."

"You didn't hear a gunshot?" Rex asked.

She shook her head. "I was wearing earplugs. Did you know they yodel at night? I wish they'd warned me about that."

"They cleared you?" I asked. "Of the murder?"

Hilly began doing jumping jacks without panting. "Turned out to be the hotel's night manager. I guess he'd been visiting this married woman in her suite across the hall for several nights until her husband surprised them both." She stopped jumping and wrinkled her face. "I can't stand that easy stuff. No one kills anyone with finesse anymore."

"And the second time?" I asked.

She rotated her arms in huge circles. "That was in Texas. I was hiding out at a dude ranch, and this guy ends up dead in my cabin. Gored. By a bull."

"In your cabin?"

"Oh wait." She paused and looked skyward. "No. Just outside of it. He'd been drunk and teasing it. The bull busted out of his pen and gored him. The guy just sort of crawled into my cabin to die. Crazy, right?"

I nodded. "Bodies turn up near me all the time too."

Hilly stopped exercising. "Hey! We should have a club! We could build a tree house and have passwords! Can we have Popsicle as the password? It's so fun to say." Then she began to do push-ups while saying the word *Popsicle* over and over.

Rex shook his head and probably rolled his eyes. I wasn't sure. He held out his cell phone with a picture of the deceased. "Ms. Vinton, have you ever seen this woman before?"

Hilly got to her feet and took the phone. Most people would be freaked out looking at a body, but to a CIA assassin (we don't have assassins) this was kind of a *meh* moment.

"I have no idea who that is," she said as she handed the phone back.

"See?" I said to Rex. "Obviously this was just some random woman who died unexpectedly in my really hard-to-get-into backyard."

Rex sighed and pocketed his phone. He kissed me on the forehead. "Nothing is ever random with you." And with that, he left.

Hilly showed no interest in the situation. She just went into the bathroom, and seconds later I heard the shower running.

I went out to the living room and sat on the couch.

Was it possible that for the first time since I'd moved here, a dead body had nothing to do with me? That would be nice. Well, not nice because someone died. But nice in the other way.

"I'm totally starving." Hilly joined me in the living room, dressed, with her wet hair in a braid. "What do you want to do for lunch? Take me to the best place in town."

There was only one answer for that.

*   *   *

"Ohmygodthisburgerisamazing!" Hilly breathed as she took another bite from her double cheeseburger.

I nodded. "Oleo's makes the best burgers in the state."

Oleo's made real food with real meat and grilled it to perfection, which meant there's lots of yummy grease. It was probably my favorite place to eat.

"You're not kidding!" She moaned. "Why is it sooooo good?"

"Corn-fed Iowa beef," I said. "Probably fresh."

Iowa was a meat and potato state. I grew up with dinner always having a meat entrée with potatoes on the side. It never got boring, and I never wanted anything else. When I was training with the CIA on the East Coast, I was shocked by the healthy eating habits there. For example, alfredo sauce should hold the weight of a standing fork, not look like wet noodles. And worse than that, nobody should eat only a salad for dinner. Ever.

"Who's that?" Hilly asked, pointing behind me. At the door.

I turned in my seat to see a young woman in her early twenties marching toward me with great purpose. Short pink hair, huge glasses with thick black frames, and about ten piercings in one ear.

"Wow," I said. "I'd hate to be whoever she's stalking."

"I think it's you." Hilly popped a handful of fries into her mouth.

Sure enough, the kid was standing over me, holding a digital recording device.

"Medea Jones," she said without extending a handshake—a serious breach of Iowan etiquette. "From the *Who's There Tribune*." She named our small-town newspaper.

"Um, hi?" I said as I wiped the grease from my hands.

"You're Merry Wrath, right?" The girl frowned.

"That's right," I mumbled.

For the last few years, I'd been kind of incognito here. When I came home, I tried to blend into the wallpaper. My last name, Wrath, was a known one here because of my mom's family. And I didn't want to deal with anyone interested in my CIA past.

That had been changing little by little as more locals learned about my story. But it was still kind of hush-hush, and I wanted to keep it that way.

"Who are you?" Medea shoved the recorder into Hilly's face. For a moment I was pretty sure she wasn't going to get that hand back.

"Hilly Vinton," my friend said.

"Hilly." Medea scowled. "Short for Hilary? Hilary Vinton?"

Hilly groaned. "I'm not Hillary Clinton. Yes, I'm aware that I look just like her. No, I'm not her." She looked at me. "Why do people always think that?"

Medea stepped back and sucked in her breath. I was pretty sure that it never crossed her mind to compare the petite, blonde, older former Secretary of State to this brunette statuesque amazon.

It was just one of Hilly's peccadillos. At some point in the last twenty years, Hilly had gotten it into her head that she was a dead ringer and often mistaken for the former First Lady. We all ignored it because she was one of the very few people in the world who could kill a man with a crazy straw.

The young reporter decided I was a bit less nuts and turned back to me. "What can you tell me about the murder victim found in your backyard today?"

Murder victim? So it was foul play. How did Medea Whoever know that already?

"Not much," I said before taking a bite of my burger. Helpful hint—food is great for stalling until you can shoot your way out of a situation.

Medea seemed to think I was going to say more than that. I wasn't.

"Did you kill the victim?" she asked.

I shook my head and took a sip of my pop.

"How did you find out that it's murder?" I asked.

"I have my sources!" the young woman snapped. "You're kind of a mystery here," she continued. Then she bent down and closed the distance, her nose just inches from mine. "I'm going to find out about you."

Medea straightened up, and after a quick glance at Hilly, whose head was cocked to the side as she stared at the kid, she turned to me again. "You're going to be my Pulitzer Prize ticket out of this town."

"I'm your what now?"

"I'm going to win print journalism's highest honor, probably in the next few months. Then it's off to the big-time!"

"New York?" Hilly asked.

Medea gave her a strange look. "No. Des Moines. *The Des Moines Register*, duh."

Hilly looked at me askance.

"Very important Iowa newspaper," I said. Turning to Medea Jones, I asked, "Why me? I'm nobody. Why don't you look for something else?"

"I've asked around to find out who the most mysterious person in town is. And everybody says it's you." She smirked as the ten piercings in her ear caught the light and blinded me.

I waved a fry at her. "How can I be the most mysterious person in town if *everybody* can tell you about me?"

A startled look crossed Medea's face, but she quickly recovered. "You moved here a few years ago. Even though your family lived here, you are an enigma. You don't have a job. Instead you volunteer with a local Girl Scout troop. And you have two houses, one right across the street from the other."

"I like to keep an eye on myself," I replied. "I hardly think that makes me mysterious." She fortunately hadn't mentioned that my dad's a very high-ranking senator and my husband is a detective.

"I'm coming after you, Merry Wrath," she snapped. "I'm going to be on you like a tick on a dog."

Well, at least she got that metaphor right.

"And I'm not giving up until I get my story!" Spinning on her heel, she stormed out of the restaurant, making me wonder what the hell had happened.

"I like her," Hilly said.

My eyes were still on the door. "Do you freelance?" I was pretty sure Medea Jones was going to be a problem from here on out.

"Nah," Hilly said. "I'm on vacation."

CHAPTER FOUR

———

Rex looked up from his desk as I barged into his office. Hilly had opted to go home for another nap. I wondered if she hibernated in between hits.

My husband greeted me with a smile and sat back in his chair. Unlike most men, he didn't mind when I dropped by the office, but he had a strict rule that we behave professionally here.

Officer Kevin Dooley walked by, his arm up to his elbow in a bag of broccoli.

I couldn't help but stare. "He's eating vegetables?"

Kevin was always eating, since his first gastro-adventure with paste as a kindergartner. I'd seen him eat almost every junk food out there, and once, he ate pickled pigs' feet while standing in the middle of a double-wide trailer meth lab. But this was new, and it scared me more than walking into a double cross in Finland. And considering that Olaf had a fifty-cal trained on me the minute I walked into the post office in Porvoo, that was saying something.

Rex followed my gaze as Dooley walked past the large window and settled at his desk. We watched as he pulled a bottle of squeezy cheese out of his desk and, after looking around surreptitiously, squirted a large amount into his mouth.

"His physical is coming up." My husband turned back to me. "Last year the doctor failed him because the test results indicated he was held together with refined sugar, salt, and processed cheese."

"Why is he still working here?" I had to ask. Kevin was a flunky who drove me nuts. Especially when he stole my food every chance he got.

Rex shrugged. "He passed the physical activity. Even got the best score ever on the 1K run."

That figured.

"So." He wiggled his eyebrows at me meaningfully. "To what do I owe this unexpected pleasure?"

Oh, right. "Why does Medea Jones know the victim in my backyard was murdered?" I dropped into a chair opposite him.

"Who thinks what?" Rex looked confused.

"Medea Jones—intrepid, ambitious cub reporter for the *Who's There Trib*."

I told him the whole story, and he listened carefully. Then he picked up the phone and called the morgue. I could hear Soo Jin's voice bubbling on the line. When he hung up, he looked at me.

"She *was* murdered. Soo Jin found a knife wound in her back that went through her heart. You said this Medea is with the newspaper?"

I nodded.

He rubbed his eyes. "I don't know how she found out. Soo Jin keeps her morgue on lockdown. And she would've told me before she told the press. She does have a couple of new guys, so maybe there's a leak?"

"I hardly think the *Tribune* qualifies as 'the press,'" I said. Then I remembered something. "If she was stabbed, why wasn't there any blood on the grass in my yard?"

"Dr. Body thinks that's because she was killed somewhere else and dumped in your yard."

"Well, that's good because it proves Hilly is off the hook."

Rex stared at me. "She's a person of interest to us here, but are you saying you originally thought…?"

I waved him off. "Riley doesn't like her. He's always been suspicious of her. It's not unusual. Handlers are a different breed. They don't like anyone, sometimes including the field agent they are working with."

"Rexley!" A squeal that could probably be heard in Bladdersly went up from the doorway, and I looked to see Rex's twin sisters, Randi and Ronni, come into the office.

Did I imagine it, or did my husband just groan?

"Hey, ladies!" I smiled, especially since they were holding a large box.

Randi, the good twin, and Ronni, evil incarnate, were taxidermists who owned *Ferguson Taxidermy—Where Your Pet Lives On Forever!* And ever since I'd met my sisters-in-law, I'd been the beneficiary of some rather odd gifts.

Lately the trend was toward fertility. Randi had decided she wanted us to have children. Immediately, if not sooner. Ronni would rather I died so she could stuff me in an embarrassing position and place my corpse prominently in her store. I suspect this because the last time I saw her, she'd asked me to smile, wave, and freeze while she took a picture of me with her cell.

Randi set the box on Rex's desk and smiled. "I'm so happy you're both here! I have come up with something special for your nursery!"

Nursery?

"Stop distracting her!" Ronni scowled at me. "She's got work to do! We can't be making you special orders for free all the time!"

She failed to mention that we'd never once asked for any of these creations.

I cast a glance at Sigurd, the stand-up comedian crow with mic, Groucho nose, and glasses. My very first piece stood on top of a bookcase in Rex's office. We couldn't have it at home. Philby would've eaten it.

Rex sighed as he leaned back in his chair. He knew better than to brush his sisters off. The best thing to do was wait to see what they had for us, *ooh* and *ahh* over it, and then hide it somewhere, preferably in the attic.

"We don't have a nursery," I started to protest.

Randi beamed at me. "Well of course you don't. But you will." She opened the box. "And when you do, you can hang this over the crib."

She pulled a large mobile out of the box. Only instead of stars or toys hanging from it, there were little dead mice dressed as angels. They were posed in various positions, with one even holding an axe and wearing an evil grin—most likely Ronni's contribution.

"Does it play music?" I asked, leaning forward to touch one of the mice.

"It does!" Randi wound up a mechanism and let it spin.

Rex cocked his head to one side. "Is that the theme song from *Unsolved Mysteries*?"

Randi clapped appreciatively. "Yes! I remember it was your favorite TV show!"

"When I was nine," Rex replied.

Through the window into the station, I spotted Hilly wandering about. She stopped at Kevin's desk, and the two regarded each other for a moment before Hilly pointed at the squeezy cheese. Kevin offered it up, and she squirted some into her mouth. They smiled at each other, and then she noticed me staring. Kevin and Hilly made a strange pairing, and possibly an unholy alliance.

"There you are!" Hilly joined us.

She stared at the mobile. After I made introductions and explained what my sisters-in-law did for a living, she turned to them.

"Can you do people?" she asked.

Randi smiled. "No. That would be illegal. But you'd be surprised how many times we are asked."

My jaw dropped. "People ask you that?"

Ronni snapped, "Of course they do!" She gave me a grin similar to axe-murder-angel-mouse. "Personally, I think it's a fair question."

Rex got to his feet. "Thanks for stopping by, ladies." He ushered his sisters to the door. "Merry and I will definitely install the mobile when the time comes."

Randi waved good-bye as Ronni scowled. In seconds, they were gone.

"Your sisters are so cool!" Hilly said as she flopped down in a chair across the desk.

"Thank you, Hilly," Rex responded.

"What are you doing here?" I blurted out.

"I was bored. What can we do now?"

I had a great idea…

* * *

"Riley Andrews!" Hilly stalked across the floor in Riley's office. "How are you, you hound dog?"

Riley had gone green and stood up, waving his hands in front of him and backing away.

Too late, because Hilly closed the gap and took his hand, flipping him onto the floor.

Riley landed like a cat but flushed deep red. Hilly was a very physical person. Tall, athletic, and great in hand-to-hand combat. She wasn't really the air-kiss type.

I thought I heard Claire snicker from her seat.

"Hello, Hilly." Riley adjusted his navy polo shirt and khaki slacks as he stood up. "I heard you were in town." He cast me a sideways glance.

"And there's been a murder!" Hilly laughed. "In Merry's own backyard!"

Riley looked at me, eyebrows raised.

I nodded. "I don't know who she was." I pulled out my phone and showed a picture to him.

He shook his head. "I've never seen her before. Looks like someone went out for a stroll and somehow got herself murdered in your proximity. Again."

Hilly clapped a hand on Riley's back, knocking him forward a couple of feet. "How's it going, big guy?" She pointed at Claire. "You sleeping with her yet?"

I turned to see Claire typing away as if she hadn't heard. I didn't know much about her, and to be honest, I'd never asked. She seemed competent, and it was Riley's business.

Hilly, however, thought differently.

Riley threw his hands up in exasperation. "No. Our relationship is purely professional."

Claire kept typing in stony silence.

"Yeah, right!" Hilly thumped him on the back, and he started to cough.

"Let's all sit down," I suggested.

Hilly always teased Riley. He didn't like her, but I don't think she felt the same way. She did, however, have his number as far as womanizing was concerned. And she called him out every chance she could.

We sat down, Riley at his desk, us across from him. No one spoke for a moment. After all, I'd just been here, but I couldn't resist bringing her here. Hilly found a glass dish of peppermints and began eating them, one by one.

"So," she said, looking like she had a mouthful of marbles, "you've gone legit!"

"I've left the Agency, if that's what you mean," Riley replied.

"And you're a private investigator?" Hilly swallowed then popped two more mints into her mouth. The pile of empty wrappers was growing.

"Yes, he is." I grinned. "Most of his cases involve following cheating spouses, but once he was hired to find a missing person."

Hilly cocked her head to one side. "Really? Like an abducted kid or something?"

Riley narrowed his eyes. "It was a husband who'd faked his death and run off."

"And"—she pointed at his chest—"you solved that?" She seemed surprised.

"I did." He sniffed. "And brought the man back to face justice."

I leaned in. "He was less than thirty miles away, hunkered down in an amusement park hotel in Altoona."

Hilly swallowed then opened another mint, depositing the wrapper on top of a pyramid of cellophane. "Sounds easy."

Riley rolled his eyes. "It isn't easy. It requires research, patience, and the guts to get it done."

Hilly shrugged. "Like I said, easy. I do stuff like that every day."

"No," he countered. "You kill a guy and throw him in the nearest dumpster."

She shook her head. "Not always the nearest. Once I had to drag a dude half a mile before I found one."

"It lacks elegance," Riley said.

"So does staking out an amusement park in a place called Altoona," Hilly countered. "Hey!" She turned to me. "Remember that abandoned amusement park we stumbled onto in Kazakhstan?"

"Of course I do," I groaned. "You were parkouring all over the place. I tried to jump over a garden gnome and twisted my ankle."

Hilly laughed. "Oh yeah! I had to carry you over my shoulder for two miles to get to a clinic!"

"You made it look easy." I nodded. "Like I weighed nothing."

She responded by jumping up and throwing Riley over her shoulder before jogging laps around the office. Claire stifled a grin, but I laughed out loud until she dropped him back at his desk.

"Still got it!" she roared.

Riley chose to act like his impression of a preppy sandbag hadn't just happened and went back to scowling at his computer monitor.

"Anyway," I interrupted before they came to blows— something I'd personally love to see. "Can you find out who this woman is, using your connections at Langley?"

Hilly's eyebrows went up. "You're using Agency databases? That's cheating."

"Send me the photo," Riley agreed. "I just got some new software I want to try out."

I fiddled with my phone and sent the image, which he downloaded. As he scrolled through his screen, Hilly looked around.

"This is nice! A real strip mall! Classy!" She whistled. "Hey!" She punched me on the arm. "I bet I could do something like this."

Riley smirked. "They kind of frown on setting up shop as a killer for hire."

"He's right." I nodded. I thought it would be kind of cool, as long as she only killed bad people…like terrorists, drug dealers, or crooked cops.

Hilly considered this for a moment. "Well, I could do something else. I could be a fishmonger. Or give sniper lessons. Or maybe I could work with Rex's sisters?"

"Wow," I answered. "You sure have a wide range of interests."

She nodded. "That comes from the job. As you take out targets, you find out about them. I've killed people from all walks of life, from a mermaid to a goatherd."

I was just about to ask about the mermaid, but she was on a roll.

"And one time my target was the largest European breeder of praying mantids."

This got my attention. "Really?"

I liked praying mantids. We found them at camp all the time. The girls were afraid at first, but once they found out that the female bit the male's head off (I didn't tell them why) and ate him, it quickly became their favorite bug.

"Do you think there'd be a need for any of those things?" Hilly asked, cocking her head to one side.

"Well," I thought out loud, "there's no real call for a fishmonger unless you like only catfish. And I can't think of how the sniper thing would be useful, except maybe to hunters. Mantids, however, are great because they eat more harmful bugs, like aphids. So, yeah. That might work."

"What if I CRISPR edited their genetics so they could shoot natural pesticides from their butts?" Hilly asked.

"When have you worked with CRISPR?" I asked.

She shrugged. "It's been a hobby of mine for a year or so."

Most people pick up knitting, or sailing, or painting. Hilly Vinton picks up gene splicing.

"What have you, um, worked on?" Please don't let it be people. Or puppies.

"It's technical, but once I spliced a tarantula with a grasshopper. But it came out weird, like a big hairy spider that could jump three feet in the air."

I tried not to visibly shudder at the thought. "I'm not sure that would be a hit."

"It would be great for scaring folks."

"Yeah, into a heart attack." Riley shook his head.

"Hey! That's not a bad idea for killing someone with arachnophobia and a bad heart!" Hilly pulled a notepad out of her back pocket, swiped a pen from the desk, and began to write.

"Mr. Andrews." Claire was right next to us, and I jumped. "I'm going out to get some office supplies."

Riley nodded as the woman walked away.

"I was wrong," Hilly mused as she stared at the young woman. "You're not sleeping with her."

"What makes you say that?"

"She's not flirty. Calls you Mr. Andrews."

Riley looked like he had no idea what to say to this.

As much as I liked seeing him squirm, I wanted to know, "Have you found the dead woman?"

His head swiveled back to the screen. "Give me a moment."

Hilly jumped to her feet and began inspecting the office. I watched as she wandered around, pulling open drawers and poking around Claire's desk. She really had no filter.

Riley didn't seem to notice her. He was deeply involved in his search.

"Found her!" he called out.

Hilly ignored him and began going through a filing cabinet.

I came around and stared over his shoulder. "Who is she?"

"Who *was* she. Her name was Anna Beth Trident. She's from DC. It says she's some sort of pharmaceuticals lobbyist."

I frowned. "What was she doing here? Any family?"

Riley shook his head. "I can't find any connection."

"Why did she show up on your special database? She sounds like a normal person."

He didn't answer, leaning toward the monitor and frowning. "Whoa. That may just be a cover. I found some stuff on a conspiracy website called *Cloak and Daggered*. They think she's a foreign agent."

"A spy?" I was getting really tired of this. Since I'd moved here, Who's There had become espionage central. It wasn't special anymore.

"For China." He looked at Hilly before beckoning me to come closer. "Merry, has it occurred to you that Hilly might be here to kill *her*?"

I shook my head. "No. If that was all, she wouldn't have made herself known. It must be some kind of coincidence. What else does the website say about her?"

He reluctantly turned back to his screen and began typing furiously. "They think she was here to steal secrets and she's really fast at it. In one day and out the next, apparently. They don't explain any more than that."

"I've got to tell Rex," I sighed. "Can you print that out for me?"

"Already emailed it to him," Riley said. "With my theory that Hilly did it."

"Hilly did what?" Hilly appeared next to us, and I jumped like a tarantula-grasshopper hybrid.

"Riley," I said, "thinks you killed the woman in the backyard. Anna Beth Trident."

"The spy for China?" Hilly asked. "Huh. Guess I should've recognized her."

Wait…what? "You know her?"

She nodded. "She's on a list at work."

"A hit list!" I said with a little too much glee. I'd always wondered what kind of paperwork went around that *particular* department. A hit list didn't seem like a surprise.

"Of course not. You know we don't do assassinations." She glanced at her phone, which was trilling. "Oh, hey, can you drop me off at your house? I need a nap."

"Your phone told you that?"

She nodded. "It's an app that tells me when to sleep. I use it on the job all the time so I get enough rest. I heard that you're supposed to sleep a lot on vacation."

"Okay," I said. "Bye, Riley."

This seemed like the perfect opportunity to grill Hilly on what she really knew. But two seconds after she shut the door, she appeared to fall asleep. I tried to talk to her but was met with silence. Was this legit, or was she avoiding answering my questions?

As I dropped her off, I couldn't help but wonder if Riley was right. Did Hilly kill Anna Beth?

I didn't go back to our place. Instead, I parked one block over where I could see Hilly's SUV in the driveway. Using my cell phone, I did a search of Anna Beth Trident and found the website *Cloak and Daggered*.

According to those conspiracy theorists, Anna Beth usually procured tech secrets. But there was some chatter that she was starting to infiltrate military bases to gain military secrets. There was a base in Des Moines, but I didn't know much about it. Was that what she was here to do?

Was Hilly here for a hit? I believed her when she said she was here to visit and take a vacation. Why would she make her presence known if she was here to do a job? That didn't make a lot of sense.

Still, why did I have this feeling gnawing at my gut that said she might truly be here for work?

I needed to make a call. Riley wasn't the only one with connections at the CIA.

Ahmed picked up on the first ring. "Do you have more cookies?" he asked excitedly.

Ahmed was one of my troop's best customers. A faithful devotee to the peanut butter sandwich cookie, he ordered by the caseload. The season had been over for months, but I always kept a stash back in case I needed intel. The guy worked in administration, but he was there and I was not, so I had to work with what I had.

"One case for one question."

"Yes." He squealed. "What?"

"Are we following a possible Chinese foreign agent named Anna Beth Trident?" I tapped on my cell. "Sending you an image now."

"She's dead? She looks dead," Ahmed said.

"She was found dead in my backyard." I didn't give him any more information than that.

"Geez! What's with you, Wrath?"

"Just answer the question."

"Hold up." Ahmed clicked furiously in the background. "I think I have something. Oh, right. Yeah. Trident was an unregistered foreign agent, which I think you know is a big no-no."

I sighed. "Yes, I do. I was a spy once, remember?"

He grumbled, "I like you better as a cookie leader."

"Ahmed, focus."

His voice went quiet. "We've been trying to find her for months. There's been some suspicion that she's hitting Midwest military bases, collecting secrets. Just last week she was sighted at the Rock Island Arsenal. The guards managed to turn her away. She never made it on post. And before that, it was the Naval Station Great Lakes in Chicago. She is kind of famous for finding intel very fast and then moving on right away. Kind of like she was in two places at once. There was some talk of her branching out into other areas, but that's just hearsay."

"In other words," I grumbled, "she was good at her job."

My heart sank. Riley was right about the spy. But was he right about Hilly too?

"There's another five boxes in it for you if you can answer one more question."

I swear I heard him dancing. It probably was a red flag that he'd sell out his country for Girl Scout cookies.

"Yes! Shoot!"

"I need to know if Hilly Vinton is here on assignment."

"That'll take a while," Ahmed said. "I'll have to hack into personnel records. It'll take some time."

"How long?"

"A day or two at best. And it'll be dangerous—you know how scary HR is."

"Text me when you've got something," I said before hanging up.

What was going on here? Was Hilly's visit just a coincidence? And why would someone like Anna Beth turn up in this small town? I was the only reason spies visited this neck of the woods. Was she here to see me?

I needed some answers. And I wasn't sure I could wait.

CHAPTER FIVE

My cell went off. It was Rex telling me he'd be late tonight because he had to follow up on a new lead. Was it Riley's tip or something else? My stomach dropped. I finally get a friend from work to visit me, and it seems as if she was here to kill someone.

Why was I surprised? *Who comes to a small town in Iowa for a vacation? Wrath! You are an idiot!*

"Hey, Merry!" Hilly knocked on my window, causing me to scream.

She opened the passenger door and climbed in. "What are you doing here?"

I smiled. "I had to run an errand. On the way back, I got a text, so I pulled over to read it. I'm into safety like that."

"Okay," she said easily. "Bad news?"

I shook my head. "Rex is just working late."

She clapped her hands. "That's great! I was thinking of a girl's night out! What do you think?"

"Oh, um, how about Des Moines?"

"How about here? After all, this is where I'm vacationing. What clubs do you have here?"

There weren't many hot spots in town, unless you considered the Corn Hole, a rednecky Iowa Hawkeyes hole-in-the-wall. I told Hilly about it, and she nodded vigorously.

"Let's go there! I haven't been in a dive bar since Baxt," she said, referring to a particularly nasty bar near Tashkent.

I laughed. "The Drunken Badger? I haven't been there since that time with you!"

She slapped me hard on the back. "Excellent! The Corn Hole it is! Now, where do I get clothes so we can blend in? I don't want to look like a tourist."

* * *

A few hours later, we stood outside the Corn Hole. Out in the country on an old gravel road, the place looked like it had been condemned in the 1980s. For all I knew, it had been.

While I wore my old *University of Iowa* sweatshirt, Hilly had taken the whole blending in thing a bit too far. She was head-to-toe black and gold. She kind of resembled a muscular bumblebee. With a gold baseball cap, black-and-gold-striped rugby shirt, black jeans, and yellow shoes, she looked like she was madly obsessed with the Hawkeyes. Come to think of it, she'd probably blend in better than I did.

We opened the door and stepped inside, waiting for our eyes to adjust to the murky bar, which smelled like body odor and pickled eggs. As usual, everyone turned toward us, evaluating us from top to bottom. Apparently we passed muster, because they went back to whatever they were doing.

"WhatcanIgetchya?" a bored middle-aged woman with a black bouffant hairdo grumbled.

"A pitcher of beer!" Hilly said enthusiastically. "Whatever everyone else is drinking."

I wasn't a huge beer drinker, but I could throw down with the best of them.

"Corn nuts and pretzels on the bar. Help yourself." The waitress walked away.

Hilly jumped to her feet and ran over, filling up a Styrofoam bowl with the snacks before running back over and sitting down.

"This is so great!" she said. "Much better fare than Baxt."

I laughed again. "That's because the snacks there were stale crackers from the Breszhnev Administration and the beer was warm and watered-down."

She cocked her head to one side. "Those weren't crackers."

I snagged a handful of pretzels. "They weren't?"

"They were broken-up shingles from the roof that had been salted to seem like crackers. Apparently the usual monthly delivery never showed up."

"I don't want to know what the beer was, then." I shuddered. The former Soviet Bloc country had seen better days, and it was no surprise that one man's roof was another man's bar snack.

"I'll never forget that night." She grinned.

"Of course you won't. That's because we got into a fight with four men."

"Who turned out to be women," she added.

It hadn't been my proudest moment. After eating a whole bowl of shingles and helping Hilly drain three pitchers of whatever, I'd had trouble thinking straight.

"In hindsight," I said between pretzels, "I probably shouldn't have tried to pet that guy's turtle."

"Woman's turtle," Hilly corrected. "How were you supposed to know that she was paranoid about her pet reptile?"

"Serves me right," I said. "Who pets a turtle?"

The scene played out in slow motion in my head. I pet the turtle. The woman grabbed my wrist and yanked, unleashing a string of Russian obscenities.

I grimaced thinking about it. "I shouldn't have called her what I did."

Hilly looked thoughtful. "A gassy llama? I thought that was pretty creative."

I shook my head. "She didn't. Punched me in the stomach."

"Yes, but we took them all out and taught them a lesson."

"What lesson?"

"Let the American pet your turtle."

I couldn't help but laugh. The waitress slammed the pitcher on the table, causing the beer to slosh everywhere. This was followed by two questionably clean, mismatched glasses. I filled both, and we toasted that memory.

"Not bad," Hilly said.

"Well, this *is* a First World country..." I mumbled into my beer.

"Do you have any cash?" Hilly jumped to her feet. "I want to play the jukebox."

I looked around. I'd been here only once before, and at that time the music was set in a loop of "Friends in Low Places." I wasn't sure they had any other songs.

I handed her my wallet anyway, because hey! I was here with an assassin. What could possibly go wrong?

I watched the crowd as Hilly walked over to the ancient and stained jukebox. She was joined briefly by a man dressed exactly like she was—and I mean exactly. They spoke for a moment, and he went back to his seat.

The strains of "Family Tradition" by Hank Williams Jr. came on. Hilly returned to her seat.

"They only have two songs," she said.

"I'm surprised they have as many as two. By the way, I saw you with your male doppelganger."

She nodded. "He invited us to join their table. I said thanks but no thanks because I'm here with my favorite gal pal."

Awwww. That was nice. "You were looking for a man for a vacation fling."

Hilly cocked her head to one side. "You're right. Maybe I should go over there. After all, he had most of his teeth."

Just then, the door swung open, and in walked a bride in a full white gown and veil. The place went quiet as she was followed by three bridesmaids in black dresses and four men in tuxes.

"Uh-oh," I muttered. I didn't want to see a bride punched in the face on her wedding day, but these people picked the wrong place at the wrong time.

"What's wrong?" Hilly asked.

"The Corn Hole isn't exactly a friendly place. It's a dive for Iowa Hawkeye fans, and they don't like having the grungy, bar fight vibe messed with. This is the last place anyone should be if they aren't wearing black and gold."

"Yeah." She craned her neck to check it out. "But aren't the bride or groom from here? Doesn't everyone know everyone in this town?"

I shrugged. "Mostly, yes. But they don't look familiar, and if they came here to slum it, they're going to get more than they bargained for. These people like a good brawl, and they don't like being treated like a novelty."

"This really is like being on vacation in a foreign place!" She grinned.

"We may have to jump in," I said to Hilly, who nodded.

The wedding party walked into the center of the room, and then there was the sound of chairs scraping on pavement as the roomful of men got to their feet. It was dead silent. But the wedding party wasn't backing down.

What were they thinking? Did the newly married couple have a death wish? This was the kind of bar where a fight broke out if you hummed the Iowa State fight song.

A couple of men dressed in ratty flannel shirts and torn jeans, each wearing a Hawkeye trucker cap, stepped in front of the bride and groom, barring their way. Angry words that I couldn't quite hear were exchanged as Hilly and I got to our feet and moved closer.

The groomsmen lined up next to the groom and, with a nod from him, whipped off their jackets to reveal black-and-gold vests embroidered with Herky the Hawkeye on them. A cheer went up, and the men went back to their seats as the bridal party approached the bar.

"That was close," I said as I plopped down into my chair.

"Does that happen a lot?" Hilly asked.

"You'd be surprised. My friend Kelly is a nurse in the emergency room. She says they get three or four victims of fights from here every night."

"So it *is* like Baxt," my friend mused.

A commotion drew our attention as we saw the bride and one of the groomsman dirty dancing on the bar.

"Hilly." I straightened in my chair. "Why are you really here?"

She looked at me blankly. "What do you mean?"

"Are you here for a job?" I shouted. The noise level had increased with the entrance of the wedding party.

"I don't need a job." Hilly shook her head as she shouted back. "I already have one. But thanks!"

The Hank Williams Jr. song was blasting now, adding to the loud singing by the wedding party in response to the lines.

"That's not what I meant!" I yelled. "I meant, are you working?"

"I don't know how to twerk!" she answered.

The noise was pounding through us at full tilt. I had little faith it would die down anytime soon.

"*Are you here to kill someone*?" I screamed, just after the jukebox cut out and an awkward silence descended. After shouting what I did, it became even more awkward.

Every head turned toward me. Even the bride looked at me curiously. In my defense, it's not like those words weren't used here on a daily basis. I guess they'd never had a woman shout that at a moment of silence.

"Way to blend in, Wrath," Hilly said out of the side of her mouth.

I gave up. "Never mind." I punched my arm into the air and shouted, "Go Hawks!"

A loud, boozy cheer went up, and the music returned. Hilly had to have heard me. She was avoiding something. I remembered that at Riley's, she hadn't shown any interest in the information on Anna Beth. Even though she'd recognized the woman and that same woman had been found dead in my backyard.

My spy-dy senses were tingling. And they were usually right.

"Let's get out of here," Hilly said.

I nodded. I threw money on the table, more than enough to settle our tab and possibly give our waitress some diction lessons, before we headed out to the car.

The fresh, wooded air was a tonic after the stinky Corn Hole. I took it in in deep gulps.

"Hilly, I—"

She cut me off. "Do you mind if we head back? I'm beat."

"Yeah, sure."

"That was some place!" she replied. "What are we doing tomorrow?"

"I have a Girl Scout meeting." At least I thought I did. I'd had a few beers and wasn't quite sure.

"Can I come?" Hilly looked like an excitable puppy.

"Of course! I was going to invite you."

I told her when I'd pick her up, and we parted ways for the evening.

Back home, Rex was already asleep.

Very quietly I climbed into bed next to him and thought about the day's events. Was Hilly working? Or was my usually overactive imagination getting the best of me? It certainly wouldn't be the first time. Or the one thousandth.

A creative mind made a spy better. It was easier to think on your feet, come up with excuses for why you were going through the drug lord's desk or how you happened to be driving around Moscow with a llama in the back seat.

But there was a dark side to it too. You tended to make up problems that weren't there. It's so easy to be paranoid when you're a spy because it's easy to think the worst. And five times out of ten, you're wrong.

Like that time in Estonia when I thought my contact's cover had been blown because she hadn't shown up for our rendezvous. Turned out she'd had a dentist appointment she'd forgotten. Or the time in Tokyo when I was convinced I'd been made by a Yakuza boss who was staring at me funny. Turned out he was having an aneurism. That was a relief.

Maybe I was reading too much into Hilly avoiding my questions. She was a bit flaky. *Fun* flaky, not *weird* flaky. It's entirely possible she just didn't understand what I was saying.

Besides, why would she kill someone, leave the body in my backyard, and then take a nap? There were dumpsters just up the street. That was her modus operandi. It was silly to think she'd kill this Anna Beth Trident in my yard.

Still…what was the woman doing here? There weren't any secrets to be had in Who's There, except for Oleo's mystery sauce for chicken fingers (it's the one thing there I won't eat). Riley said this Trident woman had been infiltrating military bases for the Chinese. But what if it was for something else?

The Chinese were notorious for intellectual property theft. They'd targeted agriculture before. That made sense. This was Iowa, so maybe she was after agricultural secrets? Special pesticides or miracle fertilizer? It wasn't a farfetched idea.

I didn't know about that at all. And this town was hardly the hub of the ag scene in Iowa. But it was a possibility. One I'd need to look into in order to rule it out. And I had an idea who could help me. I just needed to get up at the crack of dawn and be willing to drink a lot of coffee.

CHAPTER SIX

————

I was up at five in the morning and at The Café by five thirty.

"Merry!" Nels Larson called out from a table with fifteen old men surrounded by four dozen empty coffee cups. "Come join us!"

Nels had helped me out with a case last summer, and I'd learned that old dudes came here every morning to discuss what old men in Iowa think most about—the weather, the news, and why a cup of coffee isn't twenty-five cents anymore.

I joined the group, who nodded to acknowledge me. A lot of these guys were farmers, as was evidenced by their overalls and muddy boots. Nels was one of the few who lived in town and was always happy to bend someone's ear. He looked happy to see me.

A teenaged boy with a crew cut I saw once in a 1954 edition of *Life Magazine* gave me a mug, and I took a drink. I didn't like coffee, but asking for tea in this place with this particular group of men was just asking to be called a Commie.

"What are you up to these days?" Nels asked over the muffled droning of male voices. The other men had lost interest in me and had begun to discuss the nuances of open sores on pigs.

"I was just driving by and saw you in here." I smiled sweetly. "Thought I'd say hello since it's been a while."

The old guy smiled. "Well, it's always good to have someone new. I've been having coffee with these old farts for forty years now." He handed me the *Who's There Tribune*. "Especially a mystery woman."

Who Is Merry Wrath? The headline hit me like a truck. For someone who prizes her privacy, this was like walking downtown naked. The byline was, of course, Medea Jones.

I scanned the short article in horror. The photo of me grinning like an idiot must've come from my sister-in-law Ronni. How did Medea know to find one of two people in town who absolutely hated me?

Is she dangerous? Is she from Iowa? Is she really a woman?

"Oh, for crying out loud!" I gasped. "Seriously?"

Nels laughed. "I know you're a woman. I assume you're not dangerous. But I have to admit, I don't know much more than that."

I tossed the paper on the table in disgust. "Don't ever give this kid an interview. Promise?"

"I swear," he said solemnly.

I forced the story from my mind and tried to relax with small talk. We chatted for a few moments about the weather (an important topic in Iowa) before I got to the point.

"These guys are farmers, huh?" I asked innocently. "Is there anything new on the farming scene? Some big secret the seed companies don't want anyone to know about?"

Nels looked at me strangely.

I quickly added, "My family were farmers. My grandma, Adelaide Wrath, had a huge farm just outside of town. I really miss hearing her talk about it."

He smiled grandly. "I should've known, with your name being Wrath! So you're waxing nostalgic about soybeans and all that."

I nodded. "I even detasseled in the summers."

If you grew up in Iowa, you knew about detasseling. You may not have done it, but you definitely knew someone who had. Basically, the seed companies hired you to work for three weeks in July, seven days a week for twelve hours each day. You walked between two rows of corn and pulled the tassels off so the corn didn't cross-pollinate. And you hoped you'd get whips— which were the equivalent of a flower bud—and not fully opened tassels. I did it for two summers and hated it.

Nels rubbed his clean-shaven chin. "I'm not sure, but I heard there's a new fertilizer out there. Hold on." He tapped on the shoulder of the man next to him, a very large bearded man wearing a John Deere cap. So little skin showed between his hair, his bushy eyebrows, mustache, and beard that he resembled a bear.

"Hey, Erskine, what were you saying the other day about that new fertilizer?"

Erskine turned to us. I assumed he was sizing me up but couldn't tell because I couldn't see his eyes.

"Not a fertilizer," he grunted. "New corn seed. Genetically engineered to grow twice as big in half the time and acts as its own pesticide."

Now that was interesting. Maybe not to anyone outside of Iowa, but here it would be revolutionary.

"No kidding?" Nels whistled. "When did that come out?"

"It isn't out," Erskine grumped. "I'm the only test farm in the country. Got one acre of the stuff now."

Only one in the country? This guy was making my case for me.

"Yeah?" Nels asked. "How's it going so far?"

"Works like they said," Erskine said before turning back to the other men, who'd moved on from pig sores to whether it was wise to castrate said pigs because of the considerable oozing.

"That would change the industry." I tried to sound impressed and stem my gag reflex simultaneously.

Nels nodded. "Erskine has tested a lot of experimental stuff over the years."

"Isn't that risky?" I whispered.

"No." Nels smiled. "He's loaded. Hit the lottery five years back. He doesn't even need to farm anymore."

"Then why does he do it?" I asked.

Nels leaned in close and lowered his voice. "Between you and me, I think he likes the thrill of the unknown." He leaned back and then gave a startled look out the window. "Hey, does that little gal have pink hair?"

Medea Jones was storming toward the door—a woman on a mission.

"Merry Wrath!" the journalist snapped as she came to a stop next to me.

"Excuse me," I said to Nels. "I need to take this outside." And possibly kick her butt.

"See you around!" I heard him say as I grabbed the girl's arm and dragged her out to the parking lot. Once I was sure we couldn't be seen by the guys inside, I gave her my most intimidating glare.

"What's wrong with you?" I was beyond angry.

She seemed to sense that and paled, just for a moment. I wondered if anyone had ever asked her that before.

"You saw my byline." Her voice wavered for just a second.

"The whole town has seen it by now." I narrowed my eyes. "And to answer your questions, yes, I'm a native Whovian, and yes, I'm a woman."

Whovian was the term those of us from Who's There used to describe ourselves. It's a terrible nickname and often gets us confused with a certain Dr. Seuss story. But it was better than the one other suggestion brought up at a town council meeting— a Thereian.

Medea stood her ground. "The people have a right to know!"

For a brief moment I thought about kidnapping her and turning her over to the Cult of NicoDerm for a sacrifice. She was probably a legit virgin.

"What do you want?" I asked in an iron tone.

"My story," she snapped. "I know you had something to do with that murder. And I'm going to get to the bottom of it if it kills me."

I briefly considered hiring Hilly to do just that, vacation be damned.

"You don't know what you're talking about," I said. "How can you have any insight into what happened in my yard?"

Medea pushed her glasses up. "I have my sources, and I don't have to tell you who they are."

Rex might have other ideas about that.

"For your information, I had nothing to do with the deceased. Ask the police."

"Oh, sure," she sneered. "Like your husband would tell me anything that might incriminate you!"

I narrowed my eyes. "I'm not a suspect. Did it occur to you that someone dumped the woman in my yard to confuse the police?"

Oops. I didn't mean to give away the fact that Anna Beth Trident might have been killed elsewhere. Maybe this kid wouldn't notice.

"Aha!" She pulled a notebook from her messenger bag. "Detective Ferguson's wife says dead woman killed somewhere else!"

Great. I wondered if I could distract her by talking about castrating hogs with open sores.

"I didn't say that," I lied because I kind of did. "I just suggested it. Seriously, my husband doesn't talk about cases at home."

"Then why were you at the station yesterday?"

Thinking quickly, I said, "Dropping off his lunch. Are you following me?"

"And who's the brunette amazon staying at your house?" Medea went on. "Is she the killer?"

I hoped not.

"This is harassment, you know," I said. "You can't follow me everywhere and scream questions at me." Actually, she could. I just wanted to warn her off.

"It's a free country." She sniffed haughtily. "We're in a public place."

I envisioned Medea Jones in a dumpster. It made me smile.

"Look, kid, there's no story when it comes to me. Why don't you look somewhere else?"

For a split second, there was a crack in her angry façade. A single moment of doubt crossed her face before the angry mask reappeared.

"You are my story until I tell you otherwise!" she said before turning on her heel and racing across the lot to a brand new Mercedes.

So that's how it was. Entitled little rich girl wants to jump to the top of the ladder without paying her dues. And she was going to do anything to destroy me to get there.

As I drove home, a germ of an idea popped into my mind. I think I knew how to deal with Medea Jones. But first, I had to take a nap before my Girl Scout meeting.

* * *

Hilly was sitting on my porch a few hours later when I opened the door.

"Hey!" She jumped to her feet. She did that a lot. "I couldn't wait! I've been here two hours. I think I scared the mailman. Did you know your Hitler cat growls at him through the window? When's the meeting? Where are we going?"

"Back to my house," I said, worried that she'd hit my Pop-Tart stash and was overly sugared up. You might think there isn't enough sugar in them, but coat them in brown sugar and dip them in liquid chocolate... "We always meet there when school's out for the summer or holidays."

Kelly pulled up as we were walking in, and I introduced my best friend to my colleague.

"It's nice to meet you!" Kelly said with a smile.

My best friend since elementary school, Kelly was the organized, responsible yin to my disorganized, irresponsible yang. She'd been the first person I turned to when I'd decided to come home for good. And it was her idea to start the Girl Scout troop.

Besides being a nurse at the local hospital, Kelly Albers and her husband, Robert, had a little girl named Finn, after me and my real name. The toddler rarely came to meetings, so I was surprised to see her holding on to her mother's leg, grinning at me.

"It's a miniature person." Hilly jumped backwards.

I introduced the little girl, who took her thumb out of her mouth to hold out her hand to the assassin. Hilly cautiously took it, dropping it immediately and wiping her hand on her shorts.

I guessed she didn't like little kids.

Kelly did not seem to mind. At least, she didn't say anything. Probably giving Hilly the benefit of the doubt. I expected nothing less.

It didn't matter anyway because we were swarmed by ten little girls who'd somehow managed to arrive all at once. Lauren went for Finn, lifting the toddler into her arms, and began carrying her inside. The Kaitlyns led us into the house.

I had four Kaitlyns in my troop. All with last names beginning with the letter M. And after all this time, I still couldn't tell them apart. They didn't seem to mind one bit. Kelly knew who they were, and that always seemed fine. At least, I thought she did. I'd never really asked her.

Ava, Inez, Hannah, and Caterina followed Lauren, still bearing the toddler, inside. Betty followed me, staring at Hilly as if to glean the nature of her unexplained appearance. Precocious and marginally dangerous, Betty was on the fast track to becoming a spy. Her obsession with all things dark and lethal and her absolute fearlessness made me think she'd be staging coupes by age sixteen.

"Who are you?" Betty asked at last.

Hilly cocked her head to one side. "Hilly Vinton. And you are?"

"Betty."

"Betty who?"

"Let's just stick with first names for now."

Hilly turned to me. "Oh, I like this kid."

"Girls," I announced, my hand in the air, giving the quiet sign, and the girls sat in a circle on the floor. "I'd like to introduce a former colleague of mine—Hilly Vinton."

The girls perked up in their chairs. They'd found out I'd been CIA and figured out that by "former colleague," I meant *here's another spy.*

"Hello," Hilly said easily. "I'm on vacation. I've never been on vacation before."

Ava's eyes grew round. "And you came *here*?"

"Yes." Hilly looked confused. "Why? Should I have gone somewhere else?"

"If I could go anywhere on my first vacay," Ava said, "I'd go to the insurance capitol of the world—Hartfield, Connecticut."

"Insurance?" Hilly asked.

I cleared my throat. "Ava has big plans to be CEO of a national insurance agency someday."

"Well…" Hilly paused. "That's specific."

Inez raised her hand. "I'd go to London to see MI6."

Hilly waved her off. "I've been. Super boring. You should check out the Mossad in Tel Aviv, Israel. Much more interesting, and they give free Krav Maga lessons."

"Not me," Lauren said. "I'd go to Africa to see lions. I like animals."

"We want to go to a horse rescue ranch in California!" announced one of the Kaitlyns, apparently designated by the others.

Caterina and Hannah looked like they were about to speak, but Betty interrupted.

"I used to think I'd go to the Basque region or Catalan," the girl mused. "But now I think I'd like to visit one of the banana republics."

"Isn't that a store?" Hannah asked. "My mom said she used to go there in the 1980s."

Ava, who thought she knew everything, interjected, "No, it's where they sell bananas. Why would you want to go there?"

Betty rolled her eyes. "I saw it on Wikipedia. The CIA did stuff there, like a thousand years ago."

"They don't call them banana republics anymore," Hilly said. "But there are some very interesting guerilla movements down there now."

"They have gorillas in South America?" Lauren's eyes grew wide as she considered changing her earlier answer.

"Duh," Inez said. "Gorillas like bananas."

"Guerillas, not gorillas." Betty shook her head. "They're some kind of group. Like the Basque separatists."

Betty was really into revolutionary movements. It was kind of scary how devoted she was to the idea.

"Why would you want to go there?" Hannah asked. "Do they have a Disney World?"

"Or Six Flags?" Caterina asked. "I like Six Flags."

"It's all jungle," Betty said patiently. "Lots of mud and mosquitos and guns."

Hilly's eyes grew wide. "This is what they do in Girl Scouts? I wish I'd joined as a kid."

"Believe me," I answered. "Our troop is far from ordinary."

"That's because Mrs. Wrath is a spy," one of the Kaitlyns said. It was the first time any of them actually acknowledged the fact out loud in a meeting.

The room went quiet. Kelly thought this would be an excellent time for the girls to introduce themselves.

Ava stood up. She was the leader of the troop, mostly by force of will. "My name is Ava. I'm ten and like arts, crafts, and insurance."

Hannah, my peacemaker, stood up as Ava sat. "I'm Hannah," the girl said with a friendly smile. "You seem nice, and I like you."

"Caterina," was all the dark-haired little girl said. She was my quiet one.

"I'm Inez," the next girl announced. "And I'm hungry. We'd better have a good snack."

Woe be it to anyone who didn't feed my troop. Snack time was sacred, and fortunately Kelly always handled that. Mostly because I used to only bring Oreos. I guess that got old. Not to me, but someone complained.

The first Kaitlyn stood. "I'm Kaitlyn, and so are these three. We like horses." She sat down to appreciative applause by the other three, who made no effort to stand. Apparently the one Kaitlyn was enough.

Lauren did not stand because Finn had fallen asleep in her lap. "I'm Lauren. I like animals. Do you work out? You look like you work out."

Hilly nodded. "I do. Do you?"

The redhead shook her head. "No. My mom says exercise is for people who don't have lives."

Hilly cocked her head to one side. "I think your mom is right."

Betty stood up last. Crossing her arms over her chest, she asked, "Just how exactly are you Mrs. Wrath's collie?"

"Colleague," I corrected. "It's a co-worker."

Hilly opened her mouth to answer, but I cut her off. "That's enough of the introductions."

"We have a right to know." Betty stayed upright. "It's called the Freedom of Something Something Act."

I struggled not to roll my eyes. "Freedom of Information Act. I know."

"If she worked with Mrs. Wrath," Lauren said quietly from the floor, "she must be a spy. Maybe it's classified."

A hush fell over the girls as they considered this new intel.

"Anyway," I said, "Hilly is joining us today as my guest."

"I never was a Girl Scout." Hilly sat down between Kaitlyns two and three, causing a tear in the space-time continuum. "You guys will have to help me. What are you working on today?"

"Knots," Ava announced. "We work on them from time to time. It's kind of important."

"Knots? With rope?" Hilly asked hopefully.

Lauren asked, "Are you good with knots? Cuz I suck at them."

"I'm very good with knots." Hilly grinned. "Let me show you a few I use in my work."

Uh-oh…

"Merry." Kelly pulled me aside and whispered as Hilly, in only two moves, showed the girls a noose. "What exactly did your friend do at the CIA?"

"Can I get a volunteer?" Hilly asked. Every hand went up, and Hilly selected one of the Kaitlyns.

The little girl walked over, and Hilly placed the noose around her neck.

"Merry?" Kelly asked again.

"The great thing about this particular knot," Hilly said as she slid the knot around the little girl's neck, "is that it's adjustable. Meaning it can fit *anyone*!"

The girls broke out in applause.

"Who," my co-leader asked, "is she?"

"Thank you!" Hilly waved the girls off. "Now, did you know there are three other ways you can make a similar knot that will have the same results? Come over here and bring your rope."

The girls swarmed, and Hilly went to work. Lauren put the sleeping Finn on the couch and joined in.

"Merry!"

"Oh. Right. Sorry." To be honest, I didn't know about the other three ways to create a noose and kind of wanted to observe. "What was the question?"

"What kind of work did Hilly do for the CIA?"

I looked at the woman who'd been my best friend since elementary school. "She takes out targets."

Kelly narrowed her eyes. "And what are those targets exactly?" She already knew the answer. Why was she asking?

"Um, people?"

"She's an assassin?" Kelly hissed.

I shook my head. "Of course not. The CIA doesn't have assassins because that would be illegal."

Kelly, who was used to my quirks, rolled her eyes. "Yeah, I know that. But that's what she is, right?"

"Yes." I was kind of tired of denying it.

"You," she said evenly, "brought an assassin…to a Girl Scout meeting…to teach the girls how to make nooses."

"No! I mean, I brought her here, yes. But I forgot we were working on knots. So it's actually kind of your fault."

"How is this my fault?" my co-leader asked quietly as she watched Hilly move on to garrotes.

"Um, because you picked the activity?" It was true. Kelly even brought licorice for the snack so the girls could tie knots in them too.

I changed my strategy. "Well, it's educational."

"How is tying a noose that will strangle you until dead educational?"

"Well…" I thought about it. "What if there's an apocalypse and we return to a Wild West kind of lifestyle and we need to form a lynch mob?"

"Why would Girl Scouts ever form a lynch mob?"

Fortunately, I had an answer for this. "In the original Girl Scout handbook, they taught you how to stop a runaway horse and tie up a crook with only three inches of rope!" Ha! Take that!

"How many runaway horses are there in town?"

"You never know," I said. "We've had runaway chickens, ducks, and one piglet. It's only a matter of time before we have runaway horses. Which would be very dangerous, and our girls could help."

Kelly didn't say anything. She never took her eyes off Hilly. After all the years I'd talked to the kids about stuff like this, why should it bother her that Hilly was here? It wasn't like she was going to hurt the girls or anything. She'd never do that. At least, I didn't think so.

I made a mental note to make her swear she wouldn't hurt the kids.

"And then they thought I was former Secretary of State, Hillary Clinton," Hilly was saying.

"Hillary Clinton? She doesn't look anything like Hillary Clinton!" Kelly hissed.

"I know that. It's just one of Hilly's quirks."

My best friend sighed. "I am not comforted knowing that a trained assassin has quirks."

"Trained assassin?" Betty asked. She was standing next to us all of a sudden.

"I'm talking about a book I read," I said quickly. "It's about an assassin who has quirks."

"What kind of quirks?" the kid asked.

"Oh. Well, all kinds. Like eating peanut butter and banana sandwiches."

Betty levelled her gaze. "Hilly is an assassin for the CIA, isn't she?"

I shook my head. "No! She isn't! The CIA doesn't have assassins!"

The girl looked at me for a moment, as if sizing me for a dunce cap. "Okay. I'll keep your secret. But it'll cost ya."

"Are you blackmailing me?"

The girl responded by folding her arms over her chest in the iconic, universal symbol of not budging. "I want some of those chloroform wipes. Bart told me about them."

Kelly shook her head and walked over to the couch, where she picked up her sleeping daughter.

I told her to put her in my bedroom, since Hilly had the guest room.

"Your brother stole one from me and sold it to Stewie, who used it on me!" I was protective of my chloroform wipes, something I'd taken off a bad guy last month and used on Riley.

"Two wipes." Betty held up two fingers. "And I get to ask Hilly to show us how to kill a man with one punch."

"That's a lot for your silence," I said. "What do you need with chloroform wipes, anyway?"

She shrugged. "To use on my brother. Duh. Now, do we have a deal or what?"

I shook hands. What choice did I have? "But you did not get those from me. Got it? And you can't tell the other girls."

"Guess what?" Lauren shouted from the center of the huddle. "Hilly's going to teach us how to kill a man with one punch!"

"I want to renegotiate the terms," Betty said before I made her join the others.

That kid was too smart for her own good. Maybe I could distract her before she made new demands.

Kelly returned from my room in time to see Hilly pointing out the soft, vulnerable spots on Hannah.

"Snack time!" she erupted.

The girls hesitated. They were finally going to learn something cool. But on the other hand, it was snack time. In the end, their tummies won out.

"Hilly," Kelly said as the girls handed out the licorice and juice boxes. "I know you're new to this, but do you mind not teaching the girls how to kill things?"

The assassin stared off into space for a moment, her head cocked to one side. "Okay. It's a deal." Then she joined the girls.

"She had to *think* about that?" Kelly asked.

"Hey, what's up with you?" I pressed. Kelly wasn't usually so prickly.

She rubbed her face. "I've been working back-to-back shifts for the last three days. Two of the other nurses moved to Bladdersly. I'm beat."

"We lost nurses to that hellhole?"

Bladdersly was our biggest football rival. The town was like a rundown version of Who's There, and the residents were either stupid, depressed, or perpetually cranky. Probably because their football team, the Raging Bladders, sucked.

"I'm sorry," Kelly said. "I haven't been very nice to your friend." That's when I noticed the dark circles under her eyes.

"Why don't you go take a nap with Finn?" I said. "I promise, no more weird stuff. We'll go out in the yard and play games or something for the rest of the meeting."

"Deal!" Kelly said before turning and running down the hallway, closing the door behind her.

I waited until the kids and Hilly were done eating before announcing game time. Unfortunately, the girls filed out my kitchen door into the backyard instead of the front yard before I could stop them.

"Whoa! Crime scene tape!" Ava shrieked as the girls ran over to the spot where Anna Beth's body was found.

Oops. I should've taken that down.

"Who died here?" Lauren asked.

"Did you kill them?" Betty turned to Hilly expectantly.

I held my hands up. "I was just playing with crime tape," I lied.

"Looks legit to me," Betty insisted. "There's even an impression in the grass where the body was."

The girls gasped as they crowded around.

Hilly grinned. "These girls are awesome!"

I thought about Kelly in the bedroom. Did something like this qualify as too weird?

"How come there's no blood?" Inez asked.

"Because"—Ava rolled her eyes—"the forensics team cleaned it up."

That turned into a heated discussion on whether you could clean blood out of grass. One of the Kaitlyns was winning with her theory of using a toothbrush, when Hilly joined them.

"Did you know," she said, "that when you die, your blood stops pumping and eventually drains to whichever side is facing down?"

She lay down and faked a rather impressive death by kukri sword using a curved branch. "Then the blood simply drains downward and pools in my back!"

The girls applauded. Yeah, this was totally normal. All we needed now was someone to come charging through those bushes and scream how inappropriate this all was and…

"Merry Wrath!" Medea burst through the hedges.

Too late.

CHAPTER SEVEN

———

"Who's that?" one of the Kaitlyns asked.

"I don't like her," Hannah said. "She yelled at Mrs. Wrath."

Betty shrieked, "Let's get her!"

I grabbed the child's collar and held her back as she waved her arms furiously.

This whole scene seemed to surprise Medea, and she took two steps backward.

Maybe I should've unleashed Betty.

"What are you doing here?" I asked, my voice jumpy because of the struggling little girl I was holding. "This is private property, and you're trespassing." I meant for it to come out more menacing than it did. Instead, it sounded like I was emotional.

"Stop!" I hissed at the little girl, and magically, she stopped. I handed her over to Hilly, who took up where I'd left off, but Betty made no further move to attack the young reporter.

"Medea?" I asked again, taking two steps forward. "You aren't welcome here."

"What are you hiding?" she snapped. "I'll get to the truth!"

"What truth?" I asked. "You don't have a story. I'm nobody. And I don't know why that woman was found here."

"I'm a journalist!" Medea said, eyes blazing. "I'll find out the real story."

This chick was a broken record. For a journalist, she sure didn't have a large vocabulary.

Betty cracked her knuckles, and that's when I noticed the Kaitlyns quietly making a noose as Inez and Ava grabbed two large sticks from the yard and twirled them menacingly.

"Ladies!" I turned to the girls. "Stop arming yourselves. This is nothing."

"Maybe you can take her out?" Betty looked hopefully at Hilly.

"Nah," Hilly replied. "I'd need a work order for that. And I'm on vacation."

Medea stared at the tall athletic woman.

I had to get her out of here before the girl repeated what she'd heard about the assassin minutes earlier.

"That's an odd thing to say," the reporter said.

"Because she's an ass—" Betty started, but I clamped a hand over her mouth before she could finish.

"An ass–what?" Medea asked interestedly.

"Asshat," Hilly interjected. "I'm an asshat." She lifted her arms into the air and began dancing. "Finally! Out of the closet! Feels good!"

I was about to ask her how anyone could be a closeted asshat when I heard some strange mumbling on the other side of the hedges near where Medea came through. It kind of sounded like chanting.

Stewie and his teenage druid wannabees stepped through, dressed in black, their faces falling as they saw that I was standing. I really needed to plant some thorny vine or poison ivy in that hedge.

"Oh. You're awake," he whimpered.

"It didn't work!" the girl who'd called him Stewbutt said. "You said the spell would work!"

All four groups stared at each other: the druids in their black robes that in the daylight appeared to be bathrobes and one faded magician's cape, pink-haired Medea representing the *Who's There Tribune*, Hilly from the CIA, and my Girl Scout troop.

"You were going to kidnap me again?" I asked.

"Well…" Stewie looked to his friends for help, but they weren't interested in backing him up. "Yes? I guess so?"

"Who are you?" Medea turned her fury on this new group.

"We are Dread Incarnate!" Stewie shouted enthusiastically, wiggling his jazz hands at us.

The last thing I needed was for Medea to pick on these kids. Even I wasn't that cruel, even if they had planned to kidnap me again.

"They're with me," I said. "I'm a member of some weird adolescent cult that worships at night in the woods. You got me. There's your story."

Medea looked at the teens, who were now staring at me openmouthed.

"I'm magical," I pressed. "I can talk to birds and stuff. You should be afraid."

Hilly and the girls nodded, as if they'd known this all along. I wasn't sure if I should be grateful that they backed me up or worried that they believed I really was in a cult.

"Are we gonna be in the paper?" Stewie's eyes glowed with hope. "I am Odious the Demigod!" He turned to the kids next to him. "That's Heather; she's a demon. And that's Mike; he's a dark fairy."

"Dark wizard!" Mike corrected. "Why do you always think I'm a fairy?"

Stewie ignored him. "And that's Kayla; she's a witch. Next to her is Bryce. He's not sure what he is yet. He just moved here."

Stewie went for it, arms over his head. "And we are the Cult of NicoDerm!"

Medea's right eyebrow went up as she turned to me. "And what are *you* supposed to be?"

"I'm…" I really hoped I didn't have to be anything, and I couldn't remember what I'd told Rex when I got home the other night. "I'm complicated."

Stewie waddled over to the reporter. "Anyway, we meet in the woods north of town on Tuesday nights for our rituals. Everyone is welcome, as long as they wear costumes," he said, pointing at his bathrobe, which barely seemed to qualify.

"But," Heather the demon interjected, "we don't need any *wannabees*. Make sure you put that in your article."

The others nodded in approval.

My troop was strangely silent. This was too entertaining to ignore.

"And we demand a blood sacrifice," Mike added.

"But we don't actually kill anyone," Kayla corrected. "We want to make that clear. My mother would ground me if we did that."

Oh, well, at least there was some restraint.

Medea was silently processing this information. She seemed confused. Good.

"Let's show her!" Stewie shrieked.

The cult tried to circle all of us, but since there weren't that many of them, they decided to circle me instead. I let them because I wanted to get it over with, and hopefully Medea would follow them away.

"We are the Cult of NicoDerm," the group chanted as they walked around me. "Welcome our sacrifice so that we may fly!"

Stewie began to flap his arms, and the others followed, except for Kayla, who stopped.

"I thought we'd agreed to ask for time travel." She pouted.

"Not now!" Stewie hissed. To me he asked, "Is she taking pictures?"

I shook my head. "No, but she looks like she might be getting into it."

Medea grabbed her camera from her messenger bag but hesitated. Maybe reason was winning and she realized she was being punked.

The little girls got into a circle around the teens and started moving in the other direction, flapping their arms like Stewie as the druids started chanting, "Blood, blood, *blood!*"

Awww, that was nice. They wanted to help. Hilly's arms were in the air as if she was conducting us.

"*What are you doing?*" Kelly's voice boomed from the doorway.

The druids ignored her and kept chanting, the girls ignored her and kept circling, and Medea was still holding her camera.

"Oh, nothing…" I called out. "These guys are just going to sacrifice me for this reporter here."

Totally normal and not at all weird.

"Hey," Rex said as he stepped from behind Kelly. "I was just going to clear out that crime scene stuff…" His voice faded as he saw what was going on. "Okay. I'll just come back later."

The Kaitlyns began shouting, *"Blood!"* over and over. Betty pulled her Girl Scout pocketknife out of her shorts and threatened to kill the first person who came at me (I'd need to talk to her because this was violating the Scout safety procedures). And Hilly pulled up a lawn chair to watch. *Hey! Where'd she get that popcorn?*

Medea looked like she wanted to say something but turned and disappeared through the bushes.

All in all, a pretty average Girl Scout meeting.

* * *

About twenty minutes later we were back in the house, while Rex stayed outside and gave the druids a stern talking-to about why you shouldn't chloroform people and steal their dining room chairs. I watched from the kitchen as they slumped, nodding as they looked at his feet.

Kelly broke one of our leader rules and announced a second snack time, this one featuring a tub of Neapolitan ice cream she'd liberated from my freezer. She didn't even mind when Hilly told them how to use a spoon to maim an attacker. I had to admit, spoons make excellent weapons. Especially if you use both ends.

"I think I might have been hallucinating," Kelly said as Finn sat on the breakfast bar attempting to eat ice cream with her hands. "But it looked like you were participating in a coven of witches."

I nodded. "Druid cult. I'm kind of an honorary bird goddess."

She said nothing as she walked over to the girls and Hilly. "Okay, guys, we aren't going to mention the whole cult thingy, or killing people with spoons, or strangling things with nooses to your parents, right?"

"Pinky swear!" several girls shouted in unison.

"That seals it." I rubbed my hands together when Kelly returned.

You'd never be able to breach a little girl's pinky swear. It was ironclad. In fact, it was kind of sad that as you grew up, your promises became more flexible. If only the whole world utilized the pinky swear.

"You didn't tell them not to mention the second snack," I added. We had parents who would think buzzing the girls up on sugar twice in one meeting was a capital crime.

"It's too farfetched. Who'd believe them?" Kelly said as she took my bowl from me and finished it off.

CHAPTER EIGHT

———

By the time the girls were all picked up, Hilly told me she was calling it a night…something about missing one of her naps. My theory on her hibernating seemed more legit. After saying good-bye, I met Rex back at the house to find him ordering pizza.

I really loved that man.

He wrapped his arms around me and held me close. "I'm not going to lose you to a cult, am I?" His voice rumbled in his chest.

"I doubt it," I said, "especially since they can't really cast a spell to make people fly." If they could achieve that, I might consider it. After all, I was the bird whatever. Maybe I could fly with Mr. Fancy Pants, the king vulture I'd adopted at the local zoo. Wouldn't that be amazing!

He laughed and poured me a glass of wine, which, after almost being sacrificed by druids for the second time, I thought I rightly deserved.

"What did you say to Stewie and the others?" I asked between gulps.

"I told them that as this was their first offense and since my wife can take care of herself, I'd let it slide this time. And as long as they didn't kidnap, perform human sacrifices, or steal furniture, they could continue their…whatever that was…in the woods."

"That was nice of you." I smiled. "Sorry about trampling the crime scene. I'd meant to have the girls play in the front yard, but they were too fast."

Rex smiled. He knew my troop too well. "I'm not worried about that. I do have a question. Who was that pink-haired woman?"

"Medea Jones, intrepid reporter. I told you about her. She's still trying to find a story on me. Seems to think I murdered Anna Beth Trident."

Rex froze. "Who?"

Then *I* froze. I'd forgotten to tell Rex that Riley ID'd her.

"You know who the deceased is?" His voice was steady. My husband wouldn't judge me. He'd give me a chance to explain myself.

So I did. I told him about the Chinese spy, and even mentioned my trip to The Café and whether or not you should castrate ulcerating pigs, and about the new hybrid corn with special powers. And I apologized. A lot.

The pizza came in the middle of my apologizing. Rex paid and brought it to the dining room table, where Philby, Martini, and Leonard were waiting.

"It's okay," he said with a sigh. "You were going to tell me, right?"

I nodded vigorously. "I was! I just got caught up in all that cult stuff."

We ate in silence for a few moments. Since Kelly had eaten my ice cream, I was hungry. I made a mental note to call her and find out how she was. It wasn't like her to be so grumpy. By now she was used to all the strange baggage that came with me.

"You might have something there about Erskine and the experimental seed," Rex said as he gave a pepperoni each to the cats and the crust to the dog. "Something like that would revolutionize agriculture. I'm sure the Chinese would want that."

"So, who killed Anna Beth, and why did they move her from the murder scene to my backyard?"

"Well," he mused, "you have a strong connection to the CIA. And honestly, I'm not ruling Hilly out."

I sighed heavily.

"I'm not saying I'm going to arrest her. Just hear me out," Rex urged. "A dead foreign agent is found in your backyard right after a CIA assassin—"

"Who's not an assassin," I added quickly.

He continued, "—shows up out of the blue and stays at your house, the very house where the body was found? And the victim is a known, international spy?"

I took another slice. "I know it seems obvious. I'd think so too. But I don't think it's Hilly."

"But Riley does," Rex said. "You just told me that."

"Yes, I did. But not so you could hold it against me. He's never liked her."

"Look." Rex's tone changed to soothe. "I don't have any evidence against Hilly. But sooner or later we will find the original murder site. And then I might have something on her."

"You won't be able to arrest Hilly." I shook my head. "The CIA will come get her and close ranks. You know that."

Rex rubbed his forehead. "I realize that. I don't care about arresting her. I just want to close out my case."

Philby, tired of getting nothing from me (because I have a strict policy on sharing pepperoni, which is that I don't), came over and placed her paw on my pizza before sitting next to my plate with a smug look on her face. This tactic rarely worked on me, but I'd lost my appetite. I tossed her a few pepperonis (Martini had fallen asleep inside the pizza box lid) and gave the rest to Leonard.

"But I do wonder," Rex mused. "why the CIA would act domestically if it is her. I thought they couldn't do that."

I winked. "No, they don't do that."

Rex's right eyebrow went up. "Which means they do, right?"

"Look." I sighed. "It's not that confusing. The CIA doesn't assassinate people, and they don't act on domestic ground, with the exception being that they really do."

He rubbed his eyes. "Merry, how do you manage all that doublespeak?"

"They use a little shock therapy during our training," I admitted. "Enough volts to your brain, and *anything* makes sense."

His jaw dropped. "They shocked you?"

I shook my head. "Of course not. That would be illegal."

"Right." He sighed and took another piece of pizza. "I wonder if some aspects of your training might affect your ability to have children."

This time, my jaw dropped. "You want to have kids? I thought we'd discussed it!"

My chest filled with panic, and I started to hyperventilate. Don't get me wrong. I love kids—like Finn and my troop. I just wasn't ready to have any myself.

"No, I don't want to have children right now." He ran his hands through his hair. "I guess my sisters' creations are finally getting to me."

I took a deep breath. "Okay. Good. By the way"—I looked around—"where is the dead-mouse-angel mobile?"

Rex looked sheepish. "I caught Philby eating it. I swear, I just set it down on the table for one minute to answer my phone, and when I looked, three of the mice were missing."

As we turned to look at Philby, she coughed up a pair of wings and a halo. How did she do that? Obviously they had some sort of prehensile larynx that could set aside stuff to be coughed up later.

"I put it in the attic," Rex said, "with the other stuff."

"If Philby doesn't stop this," I murmured, "Ronni is going to kill her and turn her into a baby rattle."

"Or a lamp," Rex mused. "She's too fat to be a rattle."

Philby must've known what we were saying because she stuck her nose in the air and trotted across the pizza, farting as she went. She returned to her post in the living room, almost too fat to fit on the ledge, and continued her surveillance of my house.

Dinner was over.

* * *

Several hours later, once Rex was sound asleep, I got out of bed, retrieved a box of Girl Scout shortbread cookies from their hiding space beneath a floorboard in the guest room, grabbed a handful of dog treats, and headed out to the Obladi Zoo.

Yes, I'd promised Rex and the zoo director, Dr. Wulf, that I would stop breaking into the zoo at night to visit the king vulture. But it was more like a *don't ask, don't tell* policy really.

Mr. Fancy Pants, the vulture, was a troop mascot of sorts. He'd helped me nab a Yakuza boss back in DC and had been here on loan from the National Zoo for a year or so now. When I had something on my mind, he was my first stop. For a bird who ate rotting flesh, he was a very good listener.

I jumped the fence and made my way to his enclosure. I had a key I'd secretly made, and I let myself in.

"Kissing a real girl doesn't count if she's your cousin!" Dickie, the scarlet macaw, shrieked.

Robby, the kid who took care of these animals, was an awkward teenager and friend of Stewie the Demigod. Apparently he liked to complain about all the things messed up in his adolescent life while on the job, and Dickie repeated most of them.

"That crazy lady is here again!" Dickie shrieked.

I handed him a dog treat, and that shut him up. I'd tried fruit and veggies with this bird but discovered he liked these best. I had to hold some back though. I'd be paying a visit to my new friend, Wolfie, in the red wolf enclosure later.

Mr. Fancy Pants had his googly eyes fixed on me the moment I appeared. If you've never seen a king vulture, you've been missing out. They looked like something a deranged toddler would color, with a bald purple head, bright-orange wattle that hung over his beak, and two eyes that looked like they'd been glued on from a craft store.

"Hey, big fella," I said softly as I used my second illegal key to gain entry into his glassed enclosure.

The large vulture sat on his log expectantly and waited for me to open the box and crush the cookies before dumping them between us. He guzzled them down, looking a bit like Cookie Monster as he did so.

"So, I have a problem," I started. "Yet another dead body has turned up in my presence. It's a spy from China."

The bird fixed one eye on me as he continued to gobble up the crumbs.

"And I have a friend visiting from out of town who everyone thinks might be responsible. But I don't. Weird, right?"

"Stop touching that!" Dickie shrieked. "You'll get worms!"

I paused, wondering what Robby was touching that would give him worms and who had told him this.

Turning back to Mr. Fancy Pants, I opened my mouth to speak, but someone else's voice came out.

"What are we doing?" a voice whispered behind me.

I jumped into the air, spinning and landing in a defensive position.

Hilly laughed out loud.

Oh sure, scare and make fun of the spy. The assassins with the Agency were a weird sort with an unusual sense of humor. They've been known to photocopy body parts (that usually aren't their own and are, in fact, usually detached), replace all the toilet paper with sandpaper, and once this guy managed to flood the breakroom with marshmallow fluff. It took weeks to get the sticky stuff off my shoes.

"What are you doing here?" I hissed. How long had she been here? Did she hear me say she's considered a suspect?

"I followed you." Hilly sat down next to Mr. Fancy Pants, who rose up, spreading his wings in an attempt to look intimidating.

"You have a pet vulture?" she asked as she reached out and stroked one of his wings.

The bird settled down and let her. Wow. I'd never really tried to touch him before. Not like that. It wasn't out of fear. More like respect.

"I adopted him," I said a little defensively.

"Hey!" Hilly's eyes grew wide. "Is this the same bird who saved your life in DC? He's a legend!"

"Mr. Fancy Pants is a legend?" I hadn't heard that. Why hadn't I heard that?

She cocked her head to one side. "You were rescued by a bird, and everyone thinks *I'm* strange!"

What was Hilly doing here? Why was she following me? It was a bit annoying that she'd breached a sacred place. This was somewhere I went to decompress. It was like being followed into a gynecologist exam.

"Why did you follow me?" I asked.

She shrugged.

"Crazy lady has a friend!" Dickie shrieked, capturing the assassin's attention.

"Did he just…?" she started.

I let out a breath. She must've just joined me if she hadn't heard him speak earlier. Which meant she probably didn't know what I'd admitted to Mr. Fancy Pants.

"That's Dickie. He repeats everything that the teenager who cleans up in here says."

She cocked her head to one side. "Did he call you 'crazy lady'?"

I nodded. "Yup."

"So," she said, looking around, "you literally do talk to birds."

"That's right." I introduced her to Mr. Fancy Pants and Dickie. "The vulture has saved my life twice. The scarlet macaw once."

"They're just like me!" the assassin cried out. "You have a lot of people saving your life."

"Well…" I said. "It's not like it happens all the time…"

"It must if you've needed help four times!"

Okay, maybe there was a point to that.

"Maybe I should get a bird, to help with work?" Hilly got up and walked over to Dickie. The macaw stared right back at her.

I reached out tentatively and stroked the vulture's wing. He reacted the same way he had with Hilly. I think he liked it. Huh. I'd learned something new.

"Heather's super dope!" Dickie shrieked.

Hilly looked at me. "Does this kid like that weird druid girl?"

"I guess so. Budding romance in the Cult of NicoDerm."

"Which guy was he?"

I thought about that. "He wasn't there." In fact, Robby Doyle hadn't been in the woods or at my house. "Maybe he's not in the cult. Maybe he just knows her from school."

Hilly walked through the exhibit hall, pausing back in front of me and the meerkats and tortoise exhibit.

"Are those meerkats racing tortoises?" she asked.

Sure enough two meerkats were riding two turtles. The pace was slow, but they seemed ambitious. One of the meerkats appeared to be waving at us.

"They do that." I left the vulture's enclosure and locked the door. "You know what? I'm going to be really sad if they have to give this guy back to the Smithsonian someday."

"Do you do this often?" Hilly asked.

"Do what?"

"Break in here late at night to talk to birds."

"Not all the time," I said quickly. "Just when I need advice."

She walked over and stared at Mr. Fancy Pants. "He gives great advice? I could use some."

"Really?" I asked. "For what?"

"Oh, you know, the usual. Stuff like whether to stab or strangle a target…do I have to wear pants to make a kill…is too much hummus bad for me… That kind of thing."

I shook my head. "I can answer one of those now. You should always wear pants for a kill." I pictured a half-nude assassin running around. "It's more professional that way."

"And the hummus?"

I shrugged. "Works for half the world. Why not?"

She nodded in agreement. "Okay. Thanks. That really helps. He really does give good advice."

I wanted to point out that I had, in fact, been the one to give her advice. "Hey, don't mention to Rex or Kelly that I brought you here. They think I've quit my king vulture habit."

"My lips are sealed. About your best friend…"

"Kelly," I said.

She nodded. "Kelly. I don't think she likes me all that much. She didn't seem to want me at the meeting."

"It's just because you taught the girls how to kill people in interesting ways. Don't worry. She's used to it with me."

Hilly sat down on the floor, which was unusual because there were empty benches everywhere. I sat down beside her.

"It's really nice that you have a best friend. I don't have one."

I patted her arm. "Sure you do. Everyone has a best friend."

Hilly shook her head. She wasn't sad, just matter of fact about it. "I've never really encouraged that kind of thing. And on the job I work alone, so there's no real buddying up."

"What about when you were a kid?" I asked. That's how Kelly and I met.

"The other kids were boring," she said as she fiddled with the laces on her tennis shoes. "They weren't interested in the stuff I was interested in."

I wasn't entirely sure I wanted to know what she'd been interested in as a child, but curiosity got the best of me. "What were you interested in?"

"Toothpicks." She scratched her ear. "I really liked toothpicks."

"That's not so…"—yes it was—"…odd. But I have to ask. Why toothpicks?"

She shrugged. "I liked making stuff with them, like bridges, little houses, a bouncy ball."

"You made a bouncy ball out of toothpicks?" I tried to imagine how you made something round out of something straight. And how would it bounce?

"It's all in the wrist," Hilly said. "Anyway, that's all I wanted to do. I was never interested in sports, or music, or anything like that."

I eyed her athletic physique. "But you're always exercising."

She rolled her eyes. "Well, duh! I have to stay in shape. Whoever heard of a fat, lazy assassin?"

She had a point. The Japanese once had a former sumo wrestler named Ole. He could crush a man to death, but how often is that handy? And he had trouble getting through doors and running away. Not terribly efficient.

"I know!" She slapped me hard on the back. "You can be my best friend!" Hilly brightened.

Why not? I didn't think there were any rules that said I only had to have one. "Okay."

"So, what do best friends do?" The woman managed to jump to her feet without using her hands.

I had to use both hands and the wall for balance as I got up. "I guess, stuff like this. Without the breaking and entering, though."

"Right!" She smiled. "Stuff like this it is! What do we do now?"

I looked at her. "I have someone else you need to meet."

* * *

A few minutes later, I was in the fenced-in red wolf enclosure, giving Wolfie a vigorous belly rub.

Hilly refused to come in but watched from the fence.

"Come on in!" I whispered. "He's just like a dog."

"I'd rather not." Hilly shook her head. "I can't believe you have a red wolf here."

"You really are afraid of them?" I asked as I pulled a rubber ball from my pocket and threw it. The wolf raced off after it with glee.

"Maybe?" She cocked her head to one side. "Yeah, probably. I'm probably afraid of them."

"Why? Is there another reason other than what you said, that red wolves are scary?"

"I'd rather not talk about it."

"Hilly, if we're going to be best friends, you have to tell me. That's what best friends do. No secrets." If she bought this argument, then maybe she'd fess up as to why she was here.

Hilly looked both ways, squinting into the darkness. Wow. There must be a crazy reason for this. Now I had to know.

"How about this." Wolfie returned the now drooly rubber ball, and I threw it again. The wolf happily ran after it. "I'll tell you something I was afraid of once. Okay?"

"Great idea!" Hilly grinned. "Go ahead. Shoot."

Now I'd stepped in it. It shouldn't be hard since everyone's afraid of something. But this was tricky because I'd done plenty to humiliate myself over the years. Picking just the right story was key.

"Well?" she asked, folding her arms over her chest and tapping her foot.

"There are so many…" I mused, flicking through the memories I'd hidden away. "Okay. I've got one."

"Once upon a time," she said eagerly.

I shook my head. "No, this is a true story."

"I know. It's just more dramatic if it starts with 'once upon a time,'" Hilly said.

Okay. "Once upon a time, I was working in Tokyo." I didn't have to say it was classified because this was a colleague, after all. "And I had a terrifying experience with sushi."

"Sushi? You mean raw fish?" Hilly smothered a laugh.

"That's right," I said a little defensively. But in the spirit of best friends, I soldiered on. "I was eating at a dive bar, and the chef offered me up these tiny octopi. I picked one up with my chopsticks, and it began wiggling furiously. I dropped it and looked down and saw the whole bowl of tiny octopi was alive. I took the bowl and ran outside to the bay and dumped them all in the water. The chef was kind of mad about it, but I gave him a big tip. I won't eat sushi again."

Hilly nodded vigorously. "I feel the same way about dead bodies."

My eyes went wide as Wolfie dumped a very drooly ball into my hand. I tossed it again, and he ran off. "You're afraid of dead bodies? Isn't that a bit of a contradiction, considering your line of work?"

"One of my first assignments was a Mexican drug cartel leader. I had to shoot this guy, used a silencer, up close. Right through the forehead. He went down, and his eyes were open. Typical brain shot, right?"

"Right," I agreed. Head shots were always encouraged. Too many chances for your target to soldier on and come after you if you hit him anywhere else.

She nodded. "I went to grab him to dispose of him. This was before I used dumpsters. And the minute I touched him, he screamed."

"He was alive?" I gasped.

"Yes and no," Hilly answered. "He didn't move anything else. His eyes were still fixed on the sky. It was some kind of reflex action. At least, that's what my dentist said."

"I've heard of twitching but not screaming. That would've scared me stupid," I admitted.

"I thought I'd had a heart attack. Anyway, I couldn't get him to stop. It was like an air raid siren. So I punched him in the throat, and that was the end of it."

"So why the red wolf?" I felt it was time to ask.

Hilly looked at me. "I don't like the color red."

I decided not to point out that not only was she wearing red shorts, but the color red was pretty much part of her job.

"Wait." I recalled her earlier statement. "Did you say your dentist told you it was a reflex action?"

Hilly nodded, never taking her eyes off the wolf, who was now rolling around on his back as I gave him a belly rub.

"You"—I pointed at her—"told your dentist about one of your hits?" That was a huge no-no.

"Yeah. I was getting a root canal, and something he was using muddled my brain. The story just sort of came out."

People like Hilly were supposed to visit an approved dentist or doctor if they'd been put under.

"You used an Agency-approved dentist?" I asked hopefully.

She shook her head. "No. It was my cousin. He already thought I was an idiot, so he didn't believe a word of it."

Huh. I guess that would work. "What did your cousin think you did for a living?"

"Beetle dealer. He and the rest of my family believe I'm some sort of exotic insect importer."

"Really? Sounds like a sweet gig."

Hilly agreed. "I have several terrariums full of them back home. Helps with the cover."

"Who feeds them while you're away?" I wondered, worrying that my new best friend was going to go home to hundreds of dead bugs.

"Ahmed takes care of them for me. Do you know Ahmed?"

My stomach dropped. This could only be the Ahmed I had looking up her file. He'd better not talk, or he'd never eat another Girl Scout cookie.

"Yeah." I threw the ball, and Wolfie went after it. "He's my biggest cookie client."

Hilly didn't speak. She just watched as I threw the ball about a hundred times more. It was getting early. We needed to head back. With one last drooly hug, I locked up Wolfie's enclosure, and Hilly followed me out of the zoo to our cars.

"You still didn't tell me why you followed me here," I said as I unlocked my van.

She shrugged. "I was bored. I saw you leaving and decided you were up to something fun." She got into her car, gave me a little wave, and drove off.

Hilly seemed to know the layout of the town. I guessed I shouldn't have been so surprised. Spies learned very quickly how to get around, where the best avenues of escape were. It's just that she was keeping some very odd hours—sleeping most of the day, up at night.

Now that I was alone, I decided to check in on Ahmed. I took out my cell and dialed.

"Wrath?" a sleepy voice answered on the first ring. "It's five in the morning."

"You were supposed to call me back. You were going to find out if Hilly Vinton was on some sort of assignment or on vacation. Something you should know if you take care of her beetles for her."

There was a cartoon-sized gulp on the other end.

"She's out of town," he said after a moment. "She didn't say what she was doing, and I didn't ask. She's crazy. I don't want to get nosy with a crazy person."

"You should've told me you beetle-sit for Hilly."

Ahmed whined, "I just like bugs! She's got some huge rhinoceros beetles. I'm training them to carry pencils around."

In spite of the fact that I wanted to know why he would try to train a bug to deliver pencils, I decided to keep to the question at hand.

"Okay, fine. When will you know?"

The sullen voice responded, "I should know today. Delores in accounting likes mint cookies. And Andrew in communications wants those caramel thingies."

"The season is over. I'm not taking orders again until next January."

"No, these are bribes," he said. "And I'm going to need two full cases for this."

"Two cases? Are you kidding?" I exploded. How was I going to locate two cases of one of the rarest cookies in the off-season?

"Two or no deal. One of the HR administrators has been watching me. I think she knows."

"Why don't you just find out what kind of cookie she likes?" I snapped.

"I don't think you can bribe those people with anything other than the blood of virgins."

"If you don't find out what I need to know, I'll be giving them one," I warned.

"Geez. Hold your cookies. I said I'd deliver, and I will." And with that he hung up.

Maybe I shouldn't have been so hard on him. HR was the most terrifying department at the CIA, second only to the sadists/dominatrices in the travel department. And he was risking a lot for the worst cookie we sold. First thing after a quick nap, I'd have to do some searching to find those cookies. If he did deliver any intel, it would be worth it.

Five minutes later, as I slid into bed next to Rex, I couldn't shake the feeling that Hilly was up to something. I just had to find out what.

CHAPTER NINE

———

"There was another Lana sighting," Riley said an hour later.

He'd called me at the crack of dawn and asked me to come to the office. Without Hilly. Actually, he specifically insisted that I come in alone or not at all. It took some doing. Our house had a driveway and an alley with a garage with entrances to both. I slipped out the alley side and circled a couple of times on the way to make sure I wasn't being followed.

Which was silly, because at six in the morning, the only traffic in this town were the farmers headed to The Café.

I leaned over his shoulder to see a black-and-white video behind Marlowe's grocery store. Lana paced for a few seconds before walking out of view. There was no car, but it was clearly her. What was she doing there?

"I think Hilly's here to take out Lana," Riley said as the video finished.

I sat across the desk from him. "It's a good theory. Do you think she popped Anna Beth too?"

He scowled. "I don't know. Probably. I mean, she is a CIA assassin, even though they don't have assassins," he added quickly.

See? Shock treatments.

Riley continued, "I still think it's odd that Hilly shows up here when Lana is making her presence known and a Chinese foreign agent is found dead in your yard. I'm not a big believer in coincidence."

I sighed. "Me neither. What do you think Lana's doing in town? Why make her presence known now?"

"Maybe she was working with Anna Beth?" Riley asked. "Lana's always worked for the Russians, but China is an ally."

"If Hilly is in town for work," I suggested, "Lana could be trying to find out what happened to Anna Beth." I shook my head. "But that doesn't make sense. With her agent killed, she should've blown town. Lana wouldn't stick around to get killed also."

"Maybe Lana knows Hilly is here? Maybe she's going to get revenge?"

I still wasn't ruling out that Lana was hanging around to take me out. The woman had been at the edge of my life for several months now. This was just the first concrete evidence that she was really here.

"Are you going to call Langley to report Lana and Anna Beth?"

He thought about that. "If Hilly's here working, then she already has, I'm sure. So I don't think so. I'm a civilian now. I have no interest in stirring that pot."

Would Hilly report Anna Beth's murder to Langley? Had she already? It didn't negate her vacation cover, but any CIA agent would report something like that, even if on vacation.

"She followed me last night. To the zoo," I admitted. "Scared the bejeezus out of me."

"Why would she do that?" Riley asked.

"She said she was up and bored and saw me leaving in the middle of the night. I'd probably do the same thing."

"There's another theory that should occur to you." Riley steepled his hands. "Maybe you're the target. Maybe Hilly is here for you."

I really didn't want to believe that. "Why make her presence known at all? Why not just kill me and slip out of town so that no one knew she was here?"

"You said you found her behind the restaurant the other night. By the dumpsters. Maybe you busted her and she came up with this whole vacation nonsense?"

"Let's say, for the sake of argument, that you're right," I said. "That doesn't explain why Lana is making herself noticeable or why Anna Beth was here."

We sat in silence for a few moments, letting it all sink in. As much as I didn't like it, Riley made a strong argument. But even that theory had holes you could drive my van through.

"There are too many variables that connect to the CIA," he said, counting off his fingers. "Number one is you. The second is Hilly. The third is Anna Beth. The fourth is Lana. All spy related."

I groaned. "It was fun when I thought Hilly was visiting to hang out. But now I'm wondering."

"I think you need to watch your back," Riley warned. "You just called Ahmed. When do you think he'll get back to you on Hilly?"

"With *my* level of impatience?" I asked. "Yesterday. But let's cut him a break and give him a few hours."

Riley shrugged and continued searching for more information while I moved to his sofa and checked my phone. Nothing. No updates from anyone. It felt as if time had stopped. I gave Riley a quick glance.

After all of those years in the field, it was still strange to see him here, in the middle of Iowa, not scheming, bossing me around, or seducing a bevy of very willing women. For a brief moment, I'd been on the list of conquests, but then I thought he'd gone back to his old ways and dumped him.

To be honest, the romantic interest was no longer there. This man had been my closest ally and biggest pain in the butt. I'd always assumed he'd go private sector or at least back to California. But he never did.

And he never seemed to mind my barging in on him. Somewhere along the line, we'd settled into a solid friendship. Even though he'd lied to me over the past few years, I was still certain, deep down inside, that I could count on him in a pinch.

Then there was Rex. My husband was a lot like Riley in some ways—smart, sexy, funny. But he had many admirable qualities that Riley did not, like reliability, honesty, and maturity. Huh. Kelly often considered me immature. Was that why Rex and I were such a good match?

* * *

"Merry." Riley's voice echoed in the darkness.

My eyes flew open. I'd fallen asleep on the couch. On the table in front of me were a plate of Oreos and a glass of milk. That had to be Claire's doing. That woman was sharp. Riley had better not do anything to send her away.

"What time is it?" I rubbed my eyes and sat up.

"Eleven." Riley grinned. "You've been out for hours."

I munched on some cookies and took a big gulp of milk. "Did you find anything new?"

He shook his head. "No. I've hit a dead end. I think we should go to Plan B. Time to see if Ahmed has anything."

"Let's call him." I took out my cell and tapped out the number, putting the phone on speaker so Riley could hear.

"You have reached the voice mail of Ahmed Bryson," a brusque female voice said. Odd. *"Ahmed is unavailable at this time and for the foreseeable future. Have a nice day."*

"That is not good," I said slowly. "It wasn't his voice."

Riley shook his head. "That is bad. Ahmed asked too many questions. He's probably in a cell somewhere."

"Damn. He was the only one who ordered peanut butter sandwich cookies. By the case."

"Wrath," Riley said. "This could mean that Hilly is here on business."

"Yeah, I know." I slumped in the chair.

"You're up." Claire walked over a box of donuts that she deposited on the desk before going to make coffee. There were chocolate chip donuts with sprinkles, a custom order I usually had to beg the donut shop for.

The beautiful redhead gave me a bored look. "I brought these in earlier, but you were out. Considering it's nearly noon, I thought the cookies were better."

I shook my head. "Donuts for lunch are my favorite. Thanks!"

She nodded and went back to her desk. If I kept stopping by here, I was going to weigh 200 lbs. in no time.

"How does she always know what I want?" I asked as I took two out of the box.

"When it comes to junk food, you're pretty predictable," Riley said. He didn't touch the donuts. Riley was a bit of a health food nut.

"I hate this," I mumbled through a mouthful of donutty goodness. "I can't stand not knowing what's going on with Hilly." I added as an afterthought, "Oh, yeah, and Ahmed too. I hope he's okay."

Riley ignored the last part of my statement. "I know. It sucks to find out someone might not be the friend you think they are," he said. "Remember, she tried to kill you with a car bomb."

"She saved my life from a car bomb," I argued. Albeit unconvincingly. Was everything I knew about Hilly a lie?

Riley folded his arms over his chest and sat back. "She set that car bomb."

"You don't know that," I insisted. "You've never offered up any proof."

He sighed and scratched his head. "It's just a gut feeling. You remember those? They are almost always accurate."

I laughed. "You're almost always wrong! Remember that gut feeling you had about the rodeo clown in El Salvador who almost took my head off with a sword?"

"That's different," Riley sniffed. "It's hard to get a read on a man wearing clown makeup."

"How about the time you thought I shouldn't trust the daughter of the prime minister of Paraguay and she ended up giving us excellent intel?"

"How can you trust a man's daughter to give him up?"

I leaned forward so Claire wouldn't hear. "You're just mad because she dumped you."

"She didn't dump me because we weren't dating," Riley said evenly.

"Hello," Claire's voice interrupted us. "Can I help you?"

We turned to see Erskine the farmer standing there with his bushy beard and overalls.

"Need a private investigator," he said.

"I can help you." Riley stood and offered him my chair.

The man came over and sat down after I got up. If he recognized me, he didn't say so.

I sat at a table nearby to eavesdrop.

"Riley Andrews." Riley smiled and held out his hand.

"Erskine Zimmer," the man said gruffly without shaking his hand. "Need your help."

Now what were the odds that I'd run into this guy two days in a row?

"What can I do for you, Mr. Zimmer?"

"Crop was stolen."

CHAPTER TEN

————

Riley asked, "Your crop?"

"Just the experimental stuff. Other stuff's still there."

My spy-dy senses went off.

"Can you give me more detail?"

"Woke up. Whole crop of corn gone. Almost a whole acre. Every plant ripped out overnight."

"Really?" Riley asked. "Did you go to the police?"

I was wondering the same thing…after wondering how someone could take out hundreds of plants and haul them away in the middle of the night.

"Can't. Seed company wouldn't allow it. Would make the news, and this stuff's experimental."

"They don't want the news to get out that the seed exists, is that right?" Riley asked.

"Yep," was Erskine's reply.

"Any idea who did this?"

"I think it's some fool from Bladdersly. Bastards are always competing against us."

Riley thought about this. "Any idea who in Bladdersly?"

"Nope."

"Why steal every single plant?" I asked.

Erskine looked at me for the first time. "Don't know. Not like you can transplant them."

I pictured a field of corn stalks tied to sticks. Roots run six to seven feet underground. It would be impossible to transplant them.

I turned to Riley. "Can you get satellite imagery from last night?"

He started clicking away on the keyboard.

"You can help?" Erskine's bushy eyebrows went up. "I'll hire you."

Claire, sensing an important moment, led the farmer away to fill out paperwork.

Riley said quietly, "Have you ever heard of anything like this happening before?"

I thought about it. "Never. There've been a few cases where a farmer introduced root worm to destroy a crop, and one time a farmer set fire to his neighbor's crop."

"Why do that?"

"According to Grandma Wrath, the two men were competing for a seed company's test plots."

"So, that's really a thing?"

I nodded. "Riley, this seed is supposedly impervious to pests, has its own super fertilizer, and grows twice as fast. That's a huge deal. Farmers have enough to worry about with bad weather and all. This seed, if it really works, would revolutionize the industry."

He sat back and watched as Erskine walked out of the office, his paperwork filled out and a sizeable deposit paid.

"What if it was the Chinese? Their whole industry comes from industrial espionage."

"It could be," I agreed. "Anna Beth was known to work for the Chinese. Maybe they switched her from military to agricultural secrets." My mind was racing for answers. "But does it have anything to do with why she was murdered?"

Riley shook his head. "That's not my job right now. This is a big opportunity."

"Erskine Zimmer is a big opportunity?"

"His connections to the seed company are important. I could get more corporate work. That's where the real money is."

"You need work, period." I pointed at Claire. "I don't even know how you managed to hire her."

Riley looked offended. "I've made some shrewd investments lately. It's not like I need the money. I just want more work."

Riley came into money? He'd never told me that before. Shrewd investments? A monkey was better at picking out stock options. In the years we worked together, Riley only hit big in the market once, and even then, it ended up a loss.

"What shrewd investments?" I asked.

"That's none of your business," he said quickly. "You'd better go. I've got to get to work."

"But what about Lana?" I grumbled.

He waved me off. "You're on your own for a bit. This new job takes priority. The only thing I'll say is be careful around Hilly Vinton."

* * *

I left Riley with my head swimming. The theft of Erskine's crop was bizarre. I wasn't as interested in that as I was in finding Lana and learning why Anna Beth Trident was dumped in my yard and whether or not Hilly was here for the wrong reasons.

Back at home, I pulled into my driveway to see Kelly sitting on my front porch. And she wasn't alone.

"What are you doing here?" I asked as I joined my best friend, who was accompanied by Betty.

"Mrs. Albers gave me a ride," Betty said. "Can I talk to you for a moment?" She gave a surreptitious glance at Kelly. "Alone?"

Kelly smothered a grin as I walked Betty halfway around the house.

"I've got your *stuff*," Betty said quietly, like she was a dealer of some sort.

She handed me a wadded-up paper bag. Inside was the package of chloroform wipes.

"Um." I weighed the bag in my hand. "It feels a little light."

Betty nodded. "My fee."

"You asked for two wipes," I argued. "I'm pretty sure there are more than that missing."

The girl shrugged. "I can't be responsible for what's there. I had to steal it back from my idiot brother."

Great. That was all I needed. Half a package of disposable knockout drugs in the wrong hands. Of course, one pair of those hands would belong to the kid standing in front of me, and I knew she already had two somewhere for a purpose I didn't want to know about.

"Thanks." I shoved the package into the front pocket of my shorts and dragged her back to Kelly.

"Thanks for giving her a ride," I said. "Hopefully you got a good bribe out of it."

Kelly nodded but said nothing.

I tossed Betty my keys. "Run inside and check on the animals, please."

Betty took off like a rocket and slammed the door behind her. My troop loved my pets. I wasn't worried. Philby could hold her own with this girl. Probably because she was Betty in feline form.

"What's up?" I asked as I sat next to Kelly.

My best friend gave me a look that made me feel guilty for not reading her mind. I know, you think spies are really good at reading people. And I am, when it comes to lying about not being followed by guerillas or whether or not a certain terrorist is hiding drugs in a stuffed aardvark.

But when it came to peopley issues and feelings, I was never really prepared.

"Kelly, what's going on? You've been so weird lately."

She sighed heavily before nodding. "I'm thinking of quitting."

My heart stopped. "Not the troop! You can't abandon me! Those girls will *eat* me the first time I forget the snack!"

She managed a wan smile. "No, not the troop. My job. They haven't replaced the last few nurses who've left, and now I'm working constant overtime. I don't have the energy to spend time with my husband or daughter, let alone you and the girls."

I put my arm around her. Kelly was my rock. She always had been. I had to admit, I'd always been a little flaky. But Kelly was the mature one. We complemented each other. Now I had to be the rock, and I had no idea what to say.

"This week," she continued, "I've worked eighty hours already. I can't go on like this."

"Okay," I said slowly. "Well, Robert makes good money. Can't he support you for a while?"

She shrugged. "I suppose so. I haven't talked to him about it yet."

"Why not?" That was a surprise. She and Robert had an amazing marriage. I assumed they talked about everything.

"I'm afraid he'll say we can't swing it." Kelly rubbed her face.

"What about another job? Something part-time, maybe?" I suggested.

She thought about this. "I guess so. Robert couldn't argue if I had something part-time lined up. But what would I do? I've been a nurse forever. I don't know how to do anything else."

"Well…" I considered this. "What do you want to do? What would make you happy?"

She stared into space. "I have no idea. Something where I could think outside the box or be creative. I'm tired of treating people with the same injuries and viruses."

"Have you thought about working at the Girl Scout Council?" I suggested. "You're so good with kids. I'll bet they could use someone like you."

She shook her head. "I'm good with our kids. But if I had to be around them all day, I think the magic would wear off."

"Maybe Ronni and Randi could use a receptionist or office manager or something? Randi says they do mostly online orders and are always swamped." Who knew the taxidermy business was so lucrative? "And maybe if you work there, Randi wouldn't spend all her time coming up with dead animal dioramas for me."

Kelly laughed. "As tempting as that sounds, I think I'd be too skeeved out being around dead animals all day. And I don't think I have much of a head for business." A thought occurred to her. "You know, I've always loved research. Do you think Soo Jin could use me?"

I shrugged. "It couldn't hurt to ask, but you'd still be at the hospital."

She deflated. "I hadn't thought about that. I really want to try something new."

Kelly looked absolutely beat. She needed help, and beyond espionage, I didn't know what to say. I really wasn't the right one to talk to. I'd been back here for years and still had no job. Oh sure, there were a couple of offers. The mayor once suggested I could run the Who's There Historical Society for a few hours a week, but that fell through. And Riley has had an offer for me to work for him out for a while now.

Betty stuck her head out the door. "The kitchen sink's on fire. FYI." She disappeared back inside the house.

"I have to deal with that." I stood up and opened the door. "But give me a day or two. I might be able to find something."

As I found the fire extinguisher and put out the fire that Betty insisted my cat started, an idea popped into my head. Maybe I had something for her after all.

The flames died down to reveal the charred remains of a little dead mouse-angel lying pitifully in the sink. Apparently Philby had upped her game from eating them to burning them.

"What happened?" I nudged the tiny corpse. "Why didn't you just turn on the faucet?"

Betty shrugged and pointed at the cat, who appeared to be smiling maniacally. "She said not to."

Oh, well, that made sense.

CHAPTER ELEVEN

––––––––

"Come on!" I begged. "It's a great idea! She'd be a perfect fit!"

Rex shook his head. "I love Kelly, and I'd love to help her. I just don't have it in the budget."

Apparently the giant sausage and pepperoni calzone I brought him for lunch as a bribe didn't have the effect I'd hoped.

"Petition the City Council! She'd be a huge help here." I tilted my head toward the main room, where Officer Kevin Dooley was engrossed in making a cow out of transparent tape.

"That"—he nodded at Kevin—"is the perfect example of why I don't have the budget. We had to get rid of one officer last week because I don't have enough for them to do. I'm sorry, Merry."

I slumped into a chair with a sigh. This would've been great for Kelly—and for me because I'd been hoping she'd feed me information when I needed it on cases. Since pretty much 100% of murders in town had something to do with me, I thought it would be beneficial.

My husband came over to the chair and took my hands, lifting me to a standing position. He looked into my eyes. This was unusual because he didn't like displays of affection at work. I waited for him to kiss me, but he squeezed my hands.

"I'm sorry. I really wish I could help. I could call the sheriff and see if he has anything."

My eyebrows went up. Carnack's office had moved into town recently, after the old office caught fire due to faulty wiring. Since Who's There was the county seat and we had some available space downtown, it was decided that he'd set up shop here. And though I didn't usually deal with his office as much, Kelly as my well-placed spy could be good.

"Okay! Do that. Let me know!" I kissed him on the lips quickly and raced out of there before he could notice that I took the calzone with me. Finding a job for Kelly was hard work, and I was hungry.

Back at home, I'd just polished off the calzone when my doorbell rang. A quick glance across the street told me Hilly's SUV was gone. Where was she always running off to? She said she was on vacation, and if she was, it was none of my business. Still, my spy-dy senses were tingling as I opened the front door.

The man on my steps wore a fedora and trench coat. It was summer. A thick walrus mustache poked out beneath the shade of the hat.

"Ahmed," I sighed before grabbing his arm and dragging him into my house.

"How did you know it was me?" he whined.

"That's the same disguise you wore a few years back, remember?"

Ahmed had shown up on my other doorstep in disguise once before. It was a crap costume then and was a crap costume now.

"What are you doing here?" I asked as I ran around closing the drapes, knocking Philby from the windowsill.

"I escaped!" he said with a dramatic flourish, knocking his hat off in the process.

"Escaped from where?" I made him sit on the couch, where he was immediately covered in one dog and two cats.

"I like your pets," he said as he lavished attention on all three.

Leonard wriggled with delight, and Martini actually stayed awake long enough to purr before passing out on his lap. Philby glared at him from the armrest.

"Ahmed! Focus!"

"Oh, right." He took off the coat and peeled off the mustache. "Did you know HR has their own jail cells?"

I did know that. When I'd been outed, HR was most apologetic. They'd taken me to a conference room, and next to that was a dungeon. I always assumed it was used by the travel department director/part-time dominatrix for side jobs. A dungeon at the CIA would scare the hell out of anyone.

"What happened? I've been trying to get ahold of you!"

"Do you have any food?" he asked hopefully, sniffing as the scent of the calzone hung in the air.

My former colleague followed me to the kitchen, where I pulled meat and cheese from the fridge.

"Anything to drink?" His eyebrows wiggled.

I handed him a bottle of beer, and we sat at the table. Ahmed ate ravenously for a few moments, and I studied him. He didn't look any worse for wear. No bruises, and he wasn't thinner than I thought he'd be.

I waited. That was one of the most important talents for a spy. And it's one of the hardest to pull off. Many a mission has been compromised by impatient spies. And even though I was certainly impatient, I'd managed to wait. For most things. There was this time in Estonia when I was supposed to wait for a package at this hole-in-the-wall tavern. It had been seven hours late. I'd hoped the bartender didn't notice how fidgety I'd been, even though I'd eaten four dinners consisting only of Lutefisk during that time.

This was harder because whatever intel he gave me would tell me whether Hilly murdered ABT or whether I needed to start looking somewhere else. If Rex had any leads, he wasn't saying, which in hindsight, considering my past actions, was understandable.

Ahmed would determine the direction of my investigation. I wondered if he knew that. It was probably the most important thing he'd done in years. But I wasn't going to let him know that.

"I tried to be discreet," he said at long last. "But they were on to me. I might have gotten a little carried away. It's the lure of the cookies." He set his beer down. "Do you have them on you? I believe I've earned them."

I was starting to worry that Hilly would come over and see him. What would she think of Ahmed being here?

Pulling a box of peanut butter sandwich cookies from a high cupboard, I set them on the table. "Talk."

"Those HR people are insane," he said as he tore open the box. "All I did was sneak into the director's office to look for Hilly's file. I don't know how they found out!"

I groaned. "I'm sure there are cameras, Ahmed. It's the CIA!"

He nodded. "I thought about that. Which was why I promised Ben in IT a case of those caramel coconut things. He was supposed to shut down the cameras in that department."

"Just how many boxes of cookies do I owe? You were supposed to do this yourself."

Ahmed pulled a roll of paper from his pocket, and it dropped to the floor and unfurled all the way to the dining room, where Philby attacked it.

"I can't do this alone! I'm just an analyst!" he protested.

"Finish the story," I said through gritted teeth as I fought my cat for the list.

"Somehow they found out I'd been in there, and they tossed me into a cell. One of them took my phone. I thought I was a goner."

"HR doesn't usually toy with assassinations." I shook my head.

"Well, sure, I know that *now*."

"How did you get out?" I asked in spite of myself.

"Maid let me out. By the way, you owe her a case of mint cookies."

I took a moment to calm myself so I didn't implode and kill him right then and there. "It's summer! I don't have many boxes in my stash, let alone cases! We sell in February!"

He nodded. "I know. I told them that. They can wait."

That appeased me for the moment. "Did you say the maid let you out?"

"Yes. Very nice lady named Lucia."

My mind was swimming. "How would a maid have the keys to the cells?"

"Someone has to clean them." Ahmed sniffed.

I shook my head. "You didn't escape. You were *released*. They wanted to find out if you were working for some other agency." Or me.

"I came right here!" He looked around as the color drained from his face.

"Okay, so they followed you. They're probably going to be relieved you aren't working for Russia."

This didn't appease him. "I need to hide out for a little while. You have a guest room?"

I shook my head. "I can't put you up. I've got Hilly living in my old house across the street!"

Ahmed's eyes grew wide. "She's here? Like, *here* here?"

"Yes! Why do you think I asked you to find out if she's on assignment or on vacation?" I was getting more than a little frustrated and started imagining torturing him with a melon baller.

"You can't let her know I'm not watching her beetles. She'd kill me!"

"You left her prize beetles alone?" I started to worry about the bugs.

He shook his head. "No, I gave her key to Ted Vandersloot in Communications. He said he'd take care of them."

"You…" I said slowly for emphasis, "left Ted Vandersloot, who has the IQ of a pebble, to take care of a dangerous asset's pet bugs?"

Ahmed blanched appropriately. I guessed he'd never thought of that. "You need to hide me at a hotel. In your name. Preferably with room service."

"I'll put you up in one in Des Moines," I said. "It's half an hour away, and no one will ever find you. But I'm not paying for room service or digital rentals, and if I think you are for one moment taking advantage, you'll never see another Girl Scout cookie for the rest of your life."

Ahmed seemed to weigh his options. "Okay." He bit into another cookie.

"Well?" I asked.

"Well what?"

"Hilly! What is she doing here?" I shouted. "It's the reason you're on the lam!"

"Oh, that. Yeah, she's on assignment."

My heart dropped. Riley was right. She was here to kill Anna Beth, Lana, or me.

"In Bulgaria," Ahmed finished.

"Bulgaria?"

He nodded. "That's what the records say. They have no idea she's in country, let alone in Iowa."

I stood there gaping at him as he polished off the box. Had the assassin gone rogue? And what had she gone rogue for?

It was time to get rid of Ahmed while Hilly was still gone. I texted Rex to let him know I had to go to Des Moines for an "errand."

He called me back.

"That's good," my husband said. "I've actually got a meeting with Dr. Body in the morgue. She's going to give me the full report."

What? "Oh," I said. Maybe I could stash Ahmed in the basement for a few days. "I could put it off and meet you there."

"No," he insisted. "I'm sure whatever you've got is important. You go. Maybe I'll brief you later."

I hung up in frustration. This was something I wanted to know about. If only he'd hired Kelly… Of course, that would have been this afternoon, which would be kind of fast.

"Come on, Ahmed." I grabbed my purse and headed for the back door. "Grab your bag, and let's go."

The thirty-minute drive to the big city was uneventful, with Ahmed droning on and on about dung beetles. My mind was back in town at the morgue, wondering what new information was being discussed.

Which was why I stashed Ahmed at a cheap motel on the other side of the city. He didn't look happy when he found out they didn't have room service, but I gave him $100, and the pancake house next door was open 24 hours, so he couldn't complain.

"Don't open the door to anyone you don't know," I warned. "You know, the Agency might have a hit out on you." I threw that in just for fun. "In fact, don't open the door to anyone you know, either. Just to be safe."

By the time I got back, it was early evening and Rex still wasn't home. I fed the animals (ignoring Philby's usual disgust at having to eat canned food…again) and had an idea where I might find some more intel on Erskine's missing crop.

CHAPTER TWELVE

———

"Stewie!" I called out.

The gang of teen druids turned to look at me, their arms still in the air.

"I am Odious…" he shouted.

"…the Demigod," I finished. "Right. Sorry. Go ahead and finish what you guys are doing. I can wait."

The kids tried to get back into the spirit of the thing and either failed or were terrible at it.

"Oh, great Dark Lord of NicoDerm!" Stewie shouted to the heavens. Was this all the kid did all day?

"Bringer of…" Stewie paused. "Bringer of Beth!"

"It's Death, you idiot!" Heather hissed.

"Oh, great Dark Lord of NicoDerm! Bringer of Death," Stewie shouted at the sky. "Tripod of Evil!"

"It's tri-god!" Heather rolled her eyes and shook her head.

"Really?" Mike dropped his arms and looked confused. "I always thought it was tripod."

Kayla dropped her hands and put them on her hips. "It's tri-god. Why would it be a tripod?"

"Maybe he has three legs or something," Mike groused defensively. "*Stewie* thought it was tripod."

"You guys are idiots." Heather sulked. "I can't believe I gave up band camp for this."

I stayed out of it because both sides seemed to have good arguments.

Stewie gave up giving jazz fingers to the clouds and wheeled on the girls. "It's tripod! What the hell is a tri-god? That makes no sense."

"You know." Kayla rolled her eyes. "It's a guy with three heads."

"Three heads? That's ridiculous!" Stewie stamped his feet.

"It's no more ridiculous than three legs!" Heather folded her arms over her chest.

Mike piped up, "I think we can at least say we agree that the number three is involved?"

Heather had had it. "This is so stupid! We still don't have any superpowers." She ticked off her fingers. "We didn't sacrifice a virgin, and Kayla *still* hasn't taken her turn bringing snacks!"

Kayla sulked. "I brought ice cream sandwiches, but nobody ate them."

"That was a year ago, and you know the rest of us are lactose intolerant!" Heather shrieked.

Kayla made a pouty face. "How was I supposed to know that?"

Stewie looked from one girl to the other. "Well, it was in our newsletter that lactose intolerance was one of the things we wanted NicoDerm to cure."

They had a newsletter? I didn't have a newsletter! And I had more kids than they did.

"But he didn't, did he?" Kayla smirked. "I'm not bringing snacks until he does." She looked around triumphantly, as if she'd won her strange argument.

I guess we were lucky. Kelly was super organized and usually brought the snacks. We'd decided that once the girls were in fifth grade, they would pitch in. But I wasn't sure that would work. And I had no idea if any of the girls were lactose intolerant… Probably not, with the way they scarfed up ice cream.

"Maybe we should just give up," Mike said.

"Says the depressed dark fairy," Heather snapped.

"I'm not a fairy!" Mike yelled.

"Guys!" Stewie shouted. "We have to pull it together!" He pointed at me. "It's all her fault! She disrupted the sacred ceremony!"

The others turned to me, united in a cause they could understand.

"Fine," I said, walking over to join them. "Since I've already disrupted your sacred ceremony, can I ask you a question?"

There was an awkward silence. Maybe they weren't sure if I could ask?

I did anyway. "I noticed you guys have been, um, worshipping here." I pointed at the empty cornfield. "Did you guys see what happened to the corn that was there a day ago?"

The group turned toward the field as if they were seeing it for the first time.

"Hey!" Mike said. "The corn is gone!"

I nodded. "Yeah. It was here the night you kidnapped me and a few nights after that. But it has since vanished. I thought you guys might've seen—"

"*Oh My Demigod!*" Stewie jumped up and down. "We did it!"

Mike and Kayla began square dancing for some reason.

"You guys." Heather tried to get their attention. "We weren't trying to make the corn disappear."

Stewie nodded vigorously. "That's true. We must've had the wrong incantation. But hey! We made a whole crop disappear! That's something, right?"

"Right!" Mike and Kayla said in unison as they do-si-doed.

Heather nodded very slightly. "I guess so…"

Stewie ran over to her and tried to put his hands on her shoulders. Unfortunately, he was several inches shorter than her. "We're getting results! That's what's important."

"So," I said, "you didn't see whoever did this?"

Mike looked at me as if I was an idiot. "Uh, yeah! We did it. Duh!"

Kayla rolled her eyes. "She's not very smart, is she?"

"I'm right here," I said. "And I can hear you."

"Whatever." Stewie shook his head slowly. "I think it's clear that we made the corn disappear." He looked at the others and twirled his index finger at the side of his head.

"You didn't do"—I waved my hands at the field—"whatever it is you think you did. This was a theft."

The four kids froze and stared at each other. I'd drummed some sense into them at last.

"You know what that means," Stewie said.

Mike nodded. "If she's right, then it has to be!"

Heather and Kayla agreed with bobbing heads.

"What are you talking about?" I asked.

"*Aliens!*" the four shouted in unison.

There was a moment of silence—a reverent one for the kids and an I Can't Believe You Guys Are Still Alive Because You Are So Stupid one for me.

"You think aliens did this?" I asked.

"Well," Stewie said, "I'm not ruling out the idea that we made it happen, but yes. Aliens are a distinct possibility."

"You're saying," I said slowly, "that you didn't see who did this."

It was too late. The kids were holding hands and dancing in a circle, singing a song about welcoming their friends from outer space.

I got back into the van and drove off. I wasn't sure what I'd expected. It had been wishful thinking that they'd been here when the theft occurred. But it was worth a shot. They looked so ecstatic in my rearview window that I felt a little happy for them. Or at least for their delusions.

They were my last hope as far as witnesses went. Erskine had no neighbors near where the corn was stolen. No one would've seen it.

I needed more information…which was why I turned the van around and headed back.

The kids were now sprawled facedown on the ground, humming. I searched the van, but the only thing I had in my car was an empty Oreo package, which was weird because my car was usually garbage central. Maybe Rex had cleaned it out. My mess drove him crazy. You could literally eat off the floor of his car. Yes, I decided my husband had cleaned my car, so I made my way to the field.

"What are you doing?" Heather asked as I walked past.

"Checking for soil samples," I said as I scooped up some dirt and put it in the package.

"What for?" Kayla asked.

"I'm going to send them to a lab in Area 51," I answered, holding my finger to my lips.

They cheered as I drove away.

* * *

Back at home, I left my stuff on the counter for just one minute before…

"Don't eat that!" I ran across the living room and snatched the cookie packet out of Rex's hands.

"It's just broken cookie bits," Rex said. "I like the cookie part."

"No, it's not. It's a soil sample," I said before realizing what I'd said.

Rex didn't know about the corn heist because Erskine didn't want to involve the police.

"Soil sample?" he asked cautiously.

"Yeah," I lied. "As the Bird Lady of the Cult of NicoDerm, I was charged with collecting holy soil from a sacred place."

Rex closed his eyes with a brief headshake. Then he opened them and smiled. "Okay."

"Wait, you did that thing you do when you're exasperated with me," I said.

"No I didn't. I just have a small headache." He pulled his cell from his pocket and frowned at the screen. "I've got to go. Apparently there's a farmer whose crop has been stolen?"

I said nothing as he left. Had Erskine gone to the police after all? Or was it the seed company? That made more sense. I couldn't see the man paying Riley and then going to the police. If it was the seed company, what changed their mind, I wondered.

* * *

"What's with the cookies?" Soo Jin asked when I handed her the package of dirt a few minutes later. It was late, but she was still working, which was good for me.

"It's an important soil sample cleverly disguised as cookies." I winked.

The medical examiner looked confused. "Oh?"

"I need you to check the sample out."

"I'm so sorry, Merry," she soothed. "But that's not something I can do."

"You can't just look through a microscope and see evidence?" I really needed to stop binge-watching *Forensic Files*.

"No, but that does sound cool." She smiled. "What is this for exactly?"

I told her the whole story about Erskine, the druids, and that the Chinese might be involved. Since Rex was now on his way to investigate, I thought it wouldn't hurt to tell her.

On the whole, she took it pretty well.

"What do you expect to find?" Soo Jin squinted at the packet of dirt as if with this new information it might do something extraordinary.

I shrugged. "I don't know. Traces of…something?"

"Tell you what." She transferred the contents to what suspiciously resembled a urine sample cup. "I'll ask Eddie if he knows anyone who can analyze this."

I threw my arms around her. "Thanks!"

"No problem!" she said as she squeezed back. "Just don't get your hopes up, okay?"

"I won't." I hesitated in the doorway. "You had a meeting with Rex tonight about Anna Beth Trident's murder?"

Dr. Body grinned. "Yes, I did."

And…?

"Was there any new information?" I asked.

"She was killed in a cornfield. We found leaves and tassel pollen on the body in microscopic traces."

My jaw dropped. How was I going to check every cornfield around town?

"Anything else?" I hoped she'd give me the coordinates leading right to a woman-sized impression in a field, but she just shook her head. I thanked her and headed out of the hospital to the parking lot.

In the car I slammed my hand onto the dash. *Merry! You idiot! There's only one cornfield that's been involved in this investigation!* Sure, I had no idea how the corn was taken, but I'd be willing to bet that was where ABT was murdered!

As for the soil sample, what was I looking for, anyway? It wasn't supernatural or alien, that's for sure. My guess was that the Chinese government had taken the corn somehow. With their spy dead, maybe they just showed up and took the corn?

Wait a minute…was I losing my mind? This was just a theory and a farfetched one at that. Well, the alien and supernatural suggestions from the cult were a bit crazier. But still, did it make more sense that a government drove to the field in the middle of the night, took every last stalk of corn, and was able to clear out before dawn?

I still had no real, conclusive answers to many, many questions. Did Lana have a hand in this? I guess it wasn't impossible that she might work for China. Did Hilly's sudden surprise visit have anything to do with it? Why had Anna Beth been murdered? And why had she been dumped in my yard?

Argh! This was super frustrating. I did the only thing I could think of. I drove back to that empty cornfield. Hopefully Rex wouldn't be there. I needed some time to think this through.

It was getting late, but maybe I could at least find the place where the murder took place. The kids were gone when I pulled up, which was good because I had no idea what I'd say to them. This goddess thing was hard. Harder than the Girl Scouts. I mean, what were my responsibilities in that role, besides making them think aliens from outer space came down from the sky and stole sixty acres of experimental corn?

At least with them back home doing…whatever teenage druids did at this time of day, hopefully I could study the field unnoticed and without accidentally making them believe that Bigfoot or the Bermuda Triangle was involved, even if that would be pretty awesome. You had to admit, if Bigfoot had harvested a crop of experimental corn in the middle of the night, it would be fairly impressive.

As I walked through the empty furrows, once again I questioned my motives. *What was I looking for?*

The plot was large and empty. I picked my way across, my eyes sweeping back and forth, looking for anything out of the ordinary.

That's when I heard the car coming. I dove into a field of *not* stolen corn and watched as Rex and Officer Kevin Dooley parked next to my car.

Uh-oh.

Rex got out and looked into my van. He knew it was mine. There was the ketchup stain on the front passenger seat and the grease stain on the dash from a poorly placed Oleo's burger. I never was able to get those out.

To his credit, he didn't sigh or shake his head.

"Merry?" he shouted.

I didn't answer. I probably should've since I was obviously busted. But for some reason (most likely full-blown stubbornness), I held back.

Kevin was eating Cheetos out of his gun holster. Where was the gun?

Rex didn't call out for me again, just stepped into the field and looked around.

"Footprints," Kevin said, pointing with an orange index finger.

Crap. Now I was really busted. The one time Kevin does actual police work, and wouldn't you know it would lead to me.

"Merry," Rex said, finally shaking his head.

I remained hidden but noted my exit strategy. The reasonable time for coming out had passed, so it would be awkward to suddenly appear. I was committed.

The two men walked around the field, looking this way and that. After a moment Rex bent down, pulled on a pair of rubber gloves, and retrieved something from the soil. *Damn. I'd missed something.*

He motioned for Kevin to go back to the car, and the officer returned with a larger baggie. Rex hid whatever he was putting in the bag, presumably from me. Did he know I was watching?

I couldn't stand it anymore. I stood up and emerged like a true bird goddess.

"Rex?" I asked innocently. "Is that you?"

My husband straightened up and shoved the baggie behind him.

"Don't act so surprised." My husband smiled. "I know you were watching."

"What? No! I was all the way on the other side of the field. I just spotted you now." I put on my most convincing smile.

"Okay," he said. "Why are you here?"

There's a right time and a wrong time to come clean to your husband. The bad time is reserved for things like misplacing his gun when playing with it or *losing* his favorite stained shirt by *accidentally* throwing it away. The good time was when you wanted him to think you're completely innocent and didn't actually keep anything from him. That time was now.

"Riley asked me to stop by. Erskine hired him to find his crop."

Rex nodded but said nothing.

"So I was in the neighborhood and thought I'd stop by."

He looked around at the remote rural area with its winding gravel road. "In the neighborhood?" His eyebrows went up.

"Oh sure. I drive out here all the time. I just like the scenery." Too much of a stretch? In all honesty, it was somewhat true. I used to do this all the time as a teenager. I haven't done it in years, but he didn't know that.

"Why did Riley ask you?" he asked. "You haven't taken a job with him and not told me, right?"

When Riley opened his private investigator shop, he'd asked me to come work for him. I always said no because I told him with Rex as my husband, it was a conflict of interest. I wasn't 100% sure it was, but that was my answer. He still makes the offer on occasion.

I shook my head. "No. Riley just doesn't know these rural roads like I do."

"This doesn't have something to do with that soil sample you had in the cookie packet earlier, does it?"

I shook my head and lied. "Actually, that was cult business."

"Cult business?"

"Yes. Cult business. And cult rules apply here, so I can't tell you anything without invoking a demon or something."

My husband laughed in spite of himself, and I relaxed just a smidge.

"Well, someday you're going to have to confess, but I can see that today is not that day." He looked at Kevin, who was now trying to put his gun into his cheesy holster.

"Someday, I hope you'll work with me, instead of against me." He nodded toward the officer, who now pulled an orange gun out of his holster. Upon seeing the powder, he licked the blue steel. I wondered if it was loaded.

"But for right now, I have enough problems." He turned without letting me see what was in the bag. "Officer Dooley, I'm not going to tell you again. Stop licking your weapon."

"He's done this before?" I asked.

Rex nodded. "Powdered donuts last week. The gun hasn't had an accidental discharge yet, but it's only a matter of time." He gave me a wink. "See you back at home." And with that, he walked off.

CHAPTER THIRTEEN

———

The next morning found Rex and me at the breakfast table with Hilly, who'd barged in moments earlier saying she smelled bacon. Rex was frowning at the file on the dining room table. When he got up to get more coffee, I snagged the top photo.

"Oh hey." Hilly tossed me the newest edition of the *Who's There Tribune*. "Nice picture by the way."

Sure enough, there was a photo of me talking to the teen druids last night. That pink-haired nutjob was following me? The headline read, *Merry Wrath, Possible Man, Bird Goddess of Cult.*

I groaned as Rex took it from me. He started to laugh. "Medea Jones again. Says here she interviewed Stewie the Demigod."

"Ugh. There's no telling what that kid said." I dropped my head into my hands.

"He likes you." Rex read aloud, "*Mrs. Wrath can speak to birds and absolutely sees our paranormal powers!*"

"That's it." I groaned through my fingers. "That's the thing that'll get me kicked out of the Girl Scouts."

"It's not so bad." Rex tapped me on the head with the paper. "At least it's short."

I needed a distraction. I sat up and looked at the photo I'd taken from the file. Anna Beth Trident's image stared back at me accusingly.

"As for this mess, I don't get it," I mumbled. "I had nothing to do with her when I was with the CIA. And I never had any assignments in China. So why dump her in my backyard?"

Hilly said nothing. She just ate more bacon, much to Philby's chagrin. In fact, she was only eating bacon. And yet, she was in great shape. Maybe I should consider the all-bacon diet.

Rex shrugged. "The CIA is refusing to speak to us. Their spokesman told me he has never heard of her."

"Disavowed," Hilly said without looking at us.

Rex frowned. "Like *Mission Impossible*?"

"Yes. Sort of," I answered. "Basically they're denying that they've ever heard of her. But they're lying. Who's the spokesman?"

"Ted Vandersloot," Rex said.

Hilly and I sat up and stared at each other before bursting into hysterical laughter.

"You know him," Rex started.

"Oh yeah!" I rolled my eyes. "Ted's a bit of a legend—"

"—idiot legend," Hilly interrupted.

True, which was why I wasn't about to tell her he was taking care of her beetles.

I continued, "He washed out at the Farm—I've told you before about our training program. But his mother was the head of the Senate Ways and Means Committee."

"And the director owed her something big-time," Hilly added.

I stared off into space. "You know, I've always wondered what that was. It had to be something big."

"I know what it was," Hilly said.

"Well?" I shouted. "What was it?"

"The director had an ongoing affair with the prime minister of a major ally," Hilly said.

"Who?"

She shook her head. "No one you'd know."

Rex interjected, "Anyway, he couldn't have been too bad if they made him a spokesman."

I laughed. "Communications is where the CIA sends their worst. You just need to do one thing—deny everything. Any girl in my troop could do that."

Rex's curiosity peaked. "What did he do to wash out at the Farm?"

Hilly raised her arm. "Ooooh! I want to tell it! Can I?"

I nodded.

"His first time training there, during a mock shootout, he shot his partner."

"That can happen," Rex said.

"Not twenty-seven times," I added. "It was a good thing they were only paint balls. They sent him for a psych eval, and the results came back blank."

"Blank?"

I nodded. "The shrink just wrote that he had no words to describe Ted."

"The second time he went through training," Hilly continued, "he ran over his own foot with an armored car."

"That's not possible," Rex said.

I nodded. "You'd be surprised. He jumped out without putting it in *Park* or turning it off. He stood there by the window as the car kept going, and the rear tire ran over his foot."

"Do you have any idea how heavy an armored car is?" Hilly asked. "They had to replace the bones in his foot with metal ones. Which actually sounds kind of cool. Like he has a bionic foot."

"He does sound rather—" Rex searched for the right word "—ill-suited to the job."

"The third time," I started, "during the torture training, he sang like a bird before they even tied him up."

"It was really embarrassing too," Hilly added, "because he started revealing things about the head of Homeland Security that would probably null the man's security clearance."

I asked her, "Do you think it was true that he hadn't vetted his driver—who turned out to have ties to ISIS?"

"Ted was too stupid to lie. They had to shut down the exercise and pay off the trainers. One of them got a sweet assignment in the Caribbean, sitting on the beach all day."

I said, "So they moved him to PR, where he works under the watchful eye of Madame Skullcrusher."

"Madame Skullcrusher? Is that her real name?"

I shook my head. "No. It's Thelma Whitehead. But she's a ballbuster, so that's what we all call her. She actually likes it better."

"Is she incompetent too?" my husband asked.

Hilly answered "Not at all. She runs the program. You have to put someone smart in charge of idiots. We have some amazing women at work. The travel department is led by a dominatrix."

Rex nodded like he'd always suspected this before he stood up and stretched. "We've hit a dead end in Anna Beth's murder. I've interviewed most of the town, and no one had ever seen her before. She wasn't staying at either hotel in town, and she didn't visit any restaurants or get gas at the station. She's a ghost."

His cell buzzed, and he looked at it, frowning. "I've got to go. Officer Dooley brought in a jaywalker again."

"Jaywalker?" Hilly asked. "Who's Officer Dooley? The squeezy cheese guy?"

I nodded. "It's the fifth time this month. All of a sudden, Kevin wants to do his job. But the only thing he follows through on is jaywalking," I explained. "I went to school with him. He's not the brightest bulb. In fact, it's more like he's missing the whole filament."

Rex tried not to smile. "Now, Merry. You can't disrespect Officer Dooley."

"Too late. Like twenty-five years too late."

Hilly asked, "Is he really that bad?"

"He didn't talk until fourth grade. And even then he only spoke in monosyllables. In middle school, he brought a mop to the eighth-grade dance as his date. In high school, he brought a giant wheel of cheese in as his project on the Nuremburg Trials." I wiggled my eyebrows at Rex. "Shall I go on?"

He sighed. "No need. I've got to get back to the office."

"Hey!" I jumped up and followed him to the door. "What did you find in the empty cornfield?"

He gave me a look I couldn't decipher. "I don't know what you're talking about."

I narrowed my gaze. "Yes, you do. You found something and hid it behind you when I arrived."

My husband kissed me then smiled. "I'll tell you later. Especially if you don't ask."

After the door closed behind my husband, I turned to Hilly.

"You'd tell me if you were here to kill Anna Beth, wouldn't you?"

Hilly cocked her head to one side. "Merry! I'm on vacation! You can't kill someone on vacation! Everybody knows that."

"You have to see how this looks, right? You show up out of the blue, and a Chinese asset shows up dead a dozen feet away from you."

"Oh sure." Hilly nodded. "I get that. Makes total sense. In fact, now *I'm* starting to suspect me."

How was I supposed to answer that?

"Did you know that Svetlana Babikova is here?" I blurted out, trying to get a reaction.

"Who?" Hilly asked.

"Lana—the Russian agent I turned?"

"Honestly, Merry, I have no idea who you're talking about." She got up from the couch. "Now, if you don't mind, I have to go on a run."

And with that, in a T-shirt, shorts, and sport sandals, she ran out the door and down the street.

I watched as she took off down the block. It seemed like a good idea. I could use a little fresh air.

After locking the door, I stepped out onto the front stoop and took a couple of deep breaths. Hilly's responses left me less than confident. In fact, I was starting to think she might be involved after all.

It was hard to tell. Hilly was naturally…well, odd. The more I talked to her, the more confused I got. The only thing that didn't surprise me was the CIA pretending they didn't know who Anna Beth was. She was a foreign agent, and her death meant less paperwork for them.

But it was bizarre that they didn't come down here and try to close the case out in person. Was that because they sent Hilly and knew she was on the job? I really wanted to believe that she was here to take some much-needed time off.

On the other hand, if she didn't kill ABT, who did? It had to be someone who knew I lived here. Was it Lana? Now there was a thought. Lana had been hovering around for months, messing with me. Killing Anna Beth and putting her in my yard would throw suspicion on me.

Which begged the question—why was Lana still here? If she wanted revenge, why not kill me and move on months ago? Why all these minor appearances? Was she trying to drive me crazy?

It was working.

What did I know? I knew that Hilly's being here was way out of the ordinary. I knew Lana was in town and targeting me. I knew that Erskine lost a whole crop of very cutting-edge corn. I knew that Anna Beth was a spy for the Chinese—and they were partial to agricultural espionage.

Okay, so if Hilly was involved, what was she here to do? Was she here to kill Anna Beth? That seemed possible. But then, why not get the body out of town? Putting it in my backyard made waves and was noticed. That wasn't Hilly's modus operandi.

Was she here to kill Lana? That was a possibility. Granted, I hadn't had much time in the last several months to go looking for the woman, but I knew she was here. Hilly's presence could certainly be to flush out the Russian and take her out. She was on her own a lot. Like right now—she was off running somewhere.

Maybe she really was on vacation? Maybe she was here for Riley. Or me.

Climbing into my van, I found myself driving out to Erskine's field, hoping I wouldn't run into my cult out there. To be honest, the kids were starting to grow on me, but I needed to think. And I still needed to find the location where Anna Beth Trident was murdered.

As I pulled up, the furrows were just as empty as they'd been when I last was here. What did I think I'd find? I remembered that Rex had found something last night. Why didn't he tell me what it was?

With that, the fact ABT was murdered in a cornfield, Erskine's crop was missing, and Soo Jin's friend was analyzing the soil samples, I still felt that I'd missed something.

The black earth squelched beneath my feet, releasing a strong, clean scent. I know, you think it's weird that dirt should smell clean. But that's because you never smelled that deep, dark, rich Iowa soil. There's nothing like it anywhere.

I wandered aimlessly around the empty acreage, looking for something…anything that would help me solve this. But even as my mind attempted reason, I still found myself drawn back to worrying thoughts about Hilly.

Riley always thought Hilly had set the car bomb that she'd saved me from. I'd always insisted he didn't know her. But did *I* know her? What if I'd been wrong about her all this time? While I was pretty good at sussing people out, I had been wrong on occasion before.

A number of years ago in Dusseldorf, I'd totally misread a man's cues to think he could be turned as a spy, when in fact he'd been suffering from a severe iron deficiency. And in Caracas a few years after that, I'd thought this matador was trying to kill me, when in fact he just wanted to ask me out.

What I'm saying is…sometimes we get it wrong. We're spies, but we're also human. Except for Ted. He didn't have the brain power to be human.

Was I wrong about Hilly? My spy-dy sense started tingling, leaving me with a sinking feeling. I always trusted my gut, and it rarely steered me wrong. And that's when I heard something moving quickly behind me. I'd just started to turn around when a hood slid over my face and I felt the sharp, unforgettable burn of a stun gun in my side.

While most people would drop after getting hit with that kind of voltage, I had experience dealing with this type of attack. I lashed out with a punch to my assailant's stomach and was rewarded with a satisfying groan. I started to kick out toward a knee, when something smashed into the side of my head and my world slid to black.

* * *

I came to with a start, only to find myself tied down to a bed. The smelly, lumpy mattress seemed like it would be more at home in a hostel for the incontinent traveler in Thailand. My vision was obscured by some sort of hood, while my brain was pulsing to get out of my skull. As I strained against my bonds, it felt like my wrists and ankles where held fast with what seemed to be nylon rope. That hurt too, which sucked.

Great. I was good at escaping when at least my two hands were together. A situation unlike this one, where I was forced into a spread-eagle formation. And the knots held fast, telling me that Stewie and the druids weren't involved.

The scent of mildew and mold displaced the odors of the mattress, and my skin was clammy. It was as if I was in a cave or cinderblock bunker. My scrambled thoughts tried to figure out if I knew of such a place but came up with nothing. I had to be somewhere outside of town. That was bad news. Anyone looking for me would never find me.

The kidnapper was smart by taking me in the morning. Rex wouldn't even notice I was gone until evening. I was totally on my own. Like I'd been many times before over the years. The thing was, I knew what I was doing back then, and I usually knew my kidnapper. This time it could be any number of people, for any number of reasons.

Straining to listen, I heard nothing. Not even the breathing of another person. So, I was alone. That was encouraging. It was certainly easier to escape if I wasn't being watched.

"Hello?" I called out. "Is anyone there?"

Nothing.

"Hello?" I tried again. "Yoo-hoo? Kidnappers!"

Again, there was no reply.

I listened for a few moments more, just to make sure I was alone. Then I started to formulate my plan to escape. Lying here, trying to make sense of it all, was a waste of time. I had to break free and see what I had to work with.

I'd been tied up before, enough to know that this particular scenario would not be easy. I needed to calm down and think. After taking five deep breaths and letting them out, the pain fog started to thin a little. That was something at least.

Last thing I remembered I was in an empty cornfield this morning. Someone knocked me unconscious and did this to me. Had I been followed? Did I stumble onto something I shouldn't have? Or were the teenage druids stepping up their game and planning to really sacrifice me? I was kind of rooting for the latter. I was pretty sure I could take all those kids.

There was another option—maybe Rex had kidnapped me for some kinky romance. No, that wasn't right. My husband just needed to ask. He didn't have to clock me in the head and carry me off Neanderthal style.

Was this about the crop theft, or the Lana sighting, or the murder of Anna Beth Trident? Could it be all three? That train of thought wasn't encouraging because it meant I was in danger. And blindfolded and tied to a bed was not my favorite position to meet danger in.

Hey! Maybe Medea was behind this? The insane reporter finally tracked me down and was keeping me until I gave her a story. I liked that idea because I knew I could kick her butt, and I'd get the added bonus of having her arrested for assault and kidnapping.

On the other hand, why would she do something like that? She was crazy, not stupid. I ruled that theory out, regretfully. My mind was beginning to wander, and for only a second I imagined it being Rex's sister Ronni.

No, it had to be Lana or maybe even Hilly. That made me sad. It would fit with Riley's theory that Hilly really was here for me. At least I knew it wasn't Anna Beth Trident. She was dead. And so would I be if I didn't get out of here.

I tried to focus on my limbs, wiggling my fingers and my feet to see if maybe the kidnapper had done something stupid, like leave my purse where I could reach it. No such luck. How long had I been here, anyway?

Rubbing my head back and forth against the mattress made the hood loosen. Lifting my head, I telescoped it forward and up before pressing it against the mattress and dragging my head back down into its original position.

Luck at last! The hood was starting to slip! I repeated this move several times until the hood was up over the bridge of my nose. A glimmer of light where the edge was gave me hope. I *turtled* a few more times before the hood was over my forehead and I could see.

I was in a room with windows full of pieces of broken glass. From the faded, peeling wallpaper and broken window on my left, I assumed I was in a dilapidated, abandoned house somewhere in the country. Weak light streamed through the tattered remains of curtains, and I spotted dark storm clouds outside.

The room was cool, damp, and spiked with ozone. There was definitely a storm coming in. I rested my head on the mattress. Technically I was still stuck. The ropes continued to hold my arms and legs tightly.

But hey! I could see, That was something. The problem was there were maybe seven or eight abandoned houses in the countryside surrounding Who's There and many more if I was near that hellhole, Bladdersly—which, while still in the same county, existed mostly in a dimension of stupidity.

That unfortunately named town was our rival in football and competitive mouth breathing. And even though I'd known him since kindergarten, I'd always assumed Officer Kevin Dooley had at least been born there.

If I was outside of Bladdersly, I was in bigger trouble because no one in their right mind would ever think to look for me here. Did that line of reasoning mean Lana was my tormentor? She was diabolical enough to think of it. On the other hand, she wasn't from the area, so maybe not.

She was pretty resourceful though. And she'd been lurking here for months, so she could've found this place. It had to be her or Hilly. Whoever did this was dead serious about hurting me.

So, why not kill me outright? That was Hilly's job. How perfect was it for her to show up here, get me mired in a mystery so that it wouldn't be too surprising for me to vanish? On the other hand, Hilly was a friend. So maybe a friend would keep me around for a while until she decided what to do with me. I didn't know… I was still kind of new to this whole friend thing.

As for Lana, she'd been waiting a long time to come forward and claim her prize. Lana would torture and torment me, dragging out my agony for a sick, sadistic thrill. That was a sobering thought.

I really needed to get out of here.

Footsteps sounded in the near distance.

I was running out of time.

CHAPTER FOURTEEN

———

You know that saying about how your life flashes before your eyes when death is imminent? I've heard that's mostly true, but in my case, various regrets flashed before my eyes. Or at least through my mind.

I'd never celebrate my first anniversary with Rex. Never know the success from training Philby to stop smacking me randomly in the face. I'd never fulfill Randi's dream of being an aunt (not too sure if this is a regret or a relief) or Ronni's dream of me dying young in an extremely humiliating fashion. I'd never find Kelly that job. And I'd never see Betty grow up to become the greatest hitman of all time.

The steps came closer.

"Hey," I called out. "You'd better be bringing food, cuz I'm very annoying when I'm hungry."

The door squeaked. Now I faced a dilemma. Should I raise my head and look at my captor or make her come to me? While there was some small satisfaction in that, my curiosity got the better of me, and I lifted my head.

"Good afternoon, Merry." Lana smirked.

I kind of wished I'd made her come to me.

The once knockout blonde had seen better days. Her luxuriously shiny locks were now frizzy strings. She wore no makeup and was thinner than I'd remembered, which was saying something because she normally had an impossibly small waist. Even her breasts looked deflated.

"It's hard to maintain your absurdly glossy hair when you live in a place without running water, isn't it?" I smiled.

Her gaze hardened. "I can't afford to focus on little luxuries. I've been trying to get you."

"Well, here I am," I said. "And here we are, back together again. If you were going to arrange this little reunion, at least you could've brought some wine."

Lana came over and stuffed a rolled blanket that smelled like a dead goat exploded on it beneath my head and shoulders to raise me up to see. Unfortunately, this pulled on the ropes that held down my hands, giving me the excruciating sensation of being stretched on a rack.

The former Russian spy sat down on a rickety chair and grinned. "At long last, I've got you where I want you."

"Took you long enough," I grumbled.

Her once perfectly arched eyebrows rose. "I know. I just wanted to torment you. The only reason I stepped things up is because of all the spies who seem to be popping up all over town. I can't have anyone moving in on my territory, can I?"

I figured she was referring to Anna Beth, but did she also know about Hilly?

"You got me. Yay you! So, what happens now?" I asked. "You want some sort of clever conversation? Going for a little villainy monologuing, or are you going to kill me outright?"

Lana scowled. "I've waited far too long to kill you quickly. Do you know how awful that prison was? If I hadn't been able to make a shiv and a lockpick out of the underwires in my bra, I wouldn't be standing here, I can tell you that."

"That's too bad." I sighed. "You would've made some psychopathic inmate the perfect toy Barbie doll."

Inside I was impressed. I'd never thought of using a bra for anything other than strangling people. If I got out of this alive, I was going to teach my Scouts this…in a few years…when they actually needed bras.

Lana responded to my Barbie comment by getting up, coming over to the bed, and slapping me. Hard. By the way, it's always a bad idea to insult your captor. The best thing you can do is ingratiate yourself to them. The Stockholm Syndrome works wonders if the baddies think you've come around to their way of thinking.

Alas, this wouldn't work on Lana. Never in a million years would she think I'd suck up to her. And she was right.

"What exactly are we doing here?" I smiled through my stinging face and what felt like a large, red handprint on my cheek.

Lana gave me a dangerous grin. "Oh, I have big plans for you. You know, the usual. Waterboarding, red hot pokers, rusty pliers, rabid gerbils. That kind of thing."

Gulp.

"Great!" I said with as much enthusiasm as I could muster. "When do we start?"

My captor got to her feet. "Soon. I'd like to give you a little time to think about all the stupid things you've done that led you to this situation first."

As she walked away, I called out, "Well that should take about an hour at best."

She didn't have to suggest it. I was already thinking I was an idiot for assuming I was safe visiting an isolated cornfield. Or not killing her all of those times in the past when I'd had the opportunity. And switching to Coke Zero. That had been a regret *and* a disappointment.

In the distance I heard a door slam followed by a car engine. I strained to listen as it drove away, until the sound was overwhelmed by the cagey thunder outside.

That went well.

The bad news was that my wrists were killing me. The good news was that she'd left me sitting somewhat upright, so I was able to check out my surroundings. From the looks of the broken bulb overhead and the complete lack of decorative lamps, I guessed there wasn't any power here. Fortunately there was a large window that produced natural light.

Outside the sky was getting darker as more black clouds crackled with streaks of lightening. Which meant that inside the room was getting darker too. Lana had said it was afternoon, but what time?. It didn't seem possible that I'd been out that long, but maybe I'd also been drugged.

My head hurt, but I figured that was mostly due to the bludgeoning I'd gotten. There wasn't a strange taste in my mouth that sometimes comes from knockout drugs, nor was there any spot that stung from a needle.

First things first. I needed to get out of here before Lana returned with all sorts of Inquisitiony torture devices. I was not a fan of drowning, or having my fingernails ripped out, not to mention whatever she was going to do with gerbils. I needed to escape.

My purse lay in the opposite corner of the room—about as far away as Texas. Could it be possible that she left my cell phone there?

Lana looked terrible. She'd gone downhill fast. But had she gone stupid? I needed to find out.

The nylon ropes tying my bleeding wrists were becoming slick. That was good. If I ignored the pain, I might be able to get one wrist free, making it possible to escape. Unfortunately, it really, really, *really* hurt.

My right wrist seemed to have a fraction of a millimeter of wiggle room, so I leaned left, pulling as hard as I could. The pain was intense. It felt like my bones were going to break. But I didn't give up. Better this minor injury now than all the medieval horrors Lana could dream up later.

The wait was agony as seconds felt like months. Slowly but surely, my wrist began to slide a little. It took maybe twenty minutes before I was free. Wiping my wrist on my shorts, I started to work on the knot holding my left hand.

Thunder continued to tease, but there was no rain yet. And there was something else. The sound of an engine. Was Lana coming back?

In spite of my best efforts, the skin on my battered wrist continued to bleed, which made it hard to get a grip on the knot.

The unmistakable sound of the crunch of tires on gravel sent my heart into a tailspin.

The knot finally fell apart as I heard footsteps bang up the steps. I raced to get the knot on my right foot. It fell away easily, but the left one made up for that convenience by being needlessly stubborn.

The door to the house, wherever it was, opened. The knot wouldn't give at all. I wanted to scream in frustration as I heard footsteps racing up the stairs.

The last knot finally gave way, and I jumped off the bed and snatched up some wood from a broken stool next to the bed.

Standing behind the door, I tried to slow my breathing in an effort to calm down as I lifted my arm over my head, preparing to strike.

The door creaked open, and someone lingered in the doorway. From that vantage point, Lana could see that I was off the bed and with her spy background would know I was behind the door. I had to strike before she had time to think up a plan.

"*Ayaaaaah!*" I jumped into the doorway with the makeshift club over my head, only to find four little girls staring up at me.

"Betty?" I dropped my arm.

The girl smiled, as did her compatriots, Lauren, Ava, and Inez.

I blinked in case she was a mirage, but she really was there. "What are you doing here?"

Ava smiled smugly. "She *was* kidnapped! I knew it!"

Lauren shook her head. "No, Inez called it."

Ava scowled. "Yes, but I *thought* it first."

Betty stepped around me into the room. "Whoa! You were tied to the bed? What were they going to do to you? I bet something that really hurt."

Ava turned a little green.

That's when I realized my mouth was still hanging open. "How did you find me?"

Betty said, "We bugged you a year ago. Remember those earrings we gave you for your birthday?"

My hand went to my right ear. The tiny silver studs had been a gift. I'd had no idea they did anything else.

"Why on earth did you do that?" I asked, horrified and grateful at the same time.

The girl shrugged. "We had to keep tabs on you to make sure you didn't die."

That worked for me. "We have to get going. Lana could be back at any minute. And I'm guessing you guys had one of your moms bring you?"

The four girls looked at each other before shaking their heads. Had I hallucinated the car? It was possible. Maybe I'd just heard a car pull in and pull out to turn around. Happened all the time on these rural roads. Besides, why would a parent drive their kids on a rescue mission?

"You rode here on bikes?" My jaw dropped. Maybe I wasn't as far out of town as I'd thought.

"Guess again," Inez said.

"You hiked here?" I started shoving them toward the door. "Lana has a car. We really need to go, now." Preferably in time to get Rex and Sheriff Carnack out here to arrest her before she discovered I'd escaped.

"Is that blood?" Ava asked.

Before I could answer, her eyes rolled back in her head and she fell to the floor.

Betty sighed and tried to rouse her as Lauren pulled a bandana out of a backpack I hadn't even noticed she was carrying and wrapped it around my wrist in a perfect tourniquet. Inez snatched up my purse, shouldering it as she ran to look out the window.

"Guys!" she shouted. "It's raining! We have to go!"

I threw Ava over my shoulder and shoved the other three out the door.

"We have a long hike in the rain ahead of us," I said as we ran down the stairs. "And I have no idea where we are."

We burst through the front door, and I stopped dead as I took in my minivan. Betty hit unlock on the key fob and dove for the driver's side.

"*Stop!*" I shouted.

The girls stopped and turned to look at me. Ava came to and protested hanging over my shoulder, so I set her down.

"What happened?" she asked.

"You're in shock," Betty said as she decided to go for it. "I'll drive."

Lauren shook her head. "It's Inez's turn. You promised."

As the raindrops got larger and fell harder, I ran over and snatched the keys from Betty. "Get in! I'm driving!"

I peeled out of the gravel drive before the girls even had their seat belts on. Hopefully no one would report us.

"Call Rex!" I ordered Lauren, who was in the passenger seat holding my cell phone. It must've been in my purse all along.

The call went right to voice mail.

"How did you get my car from that cornfield?"

In the rearview mirror, I spotted confused looks.

"Your van was at your house," Betty said. "That's where we got it."

Ava nodded. "You shouldn't leave the keys in it unlocked. Somebody might steal it."

Lana must've driven my van back to avoid raising suspicion.

"What made you think I was in trouble?" The tires skidded a little on the slick gravel.

Betty sighed, not happy to give up her secrets. "Stewie was setting up a taco bar for visiting aliens when he saw someone carry you off. He told my brother, who told me. He was afraid some other cult was stealing their bird goddess."

Ava announced, "So we looked you up using the app on Betty's phone."

"Ava!" Inez shouted. "You weren't supposed to tell her that!"

"Enough!" I intervened. "That's not important right now because we need to get out of here."

At an intersection walled by corn, I realized where we were. Just half a mile north of town. I hit the gas and drove about twenty miles over the speed limit.

"Should I call 9-1-1?" Lauren awaited instructions.

"Absolutely," I said. "And put it on speaker mode."

"9-1-1," a bored male voice answered. "What's your emergency?"

"Kevin Dooley?" I asked in shock. "Why are you…what are you…where's the dispatcher?"

"Fell. Got hurt. Ambulance took her," came the reply.

"Where's Rex?" I asked.

"Responding to a car theft. Some neighbor of his saw some midgets stealing a van in his driveway."

I looked at the girls, who all seemed very interested in the rain that was now pounding the windows.

"Call it off. I'm driving it. There was no theft."

"Okay," he said. I thought I heard the crunch of potato chips.

"Kevin?" I asked. "Do you know who this is?"

I literally heard him shrug. "No."

"It's Merry!" I screamed.

"Okay." In the background was the unmistakable crinkle of a bag of chips.

"Kevin! I called on the emergency line! Aren't you even interested in finding out how to help me?"

"Oh. Right. What's wrong?"

"Never mind." I hung up.

"First of all," I said to my van mates, "no more tracking me via my earrings."

"We were worried about you!" Ava said.

Lauren agreed. "Betty thought you'd been kidnapped by a chainsaw killer."

Inez's hand shot up from the back seat. "I called killer clown!"

Lauren looked curiously at me. "Was it a killer clown or a chainsaw killer?"

I shook my head. "It's worse than that. But let me finish. Number two—no more stealing my car or driving until you are old enough."

There was some noncommittal grumbling from the back seat as I turned onto a blacktop road.

"And thirdly…" I relaxed a little. "Thank you."

"You're welcome," Lauren said. The others nodded in agreement.

"Are we going to the hospital?" Ava asked.

I shook my head. "No. We're going to the sheriff's office to get the big guns."

A huge cheer erupted from the back seat.

* * *

"Mrs. Ferguson?" One of the deputies came around his desk when we walked in. He spotted the ligature marks on my left wrist and ankles and then the dried blood on my arm.

"Sheriff!" he shouted.

Carnack came into the office. He looked me up and down. "Are you alright?"

I nodded but inside shook my head. "I was kidnapped. I escaped." I looked nervously at the girls, hoping they wouldn't say anything. They didn't.

"What?" Carnack looked alarmed. "When? Where?"

"I think"—I pictured the house in my mind—"I was held at the old Higgins place, off 187th."

The sheriff and his deputy strapped on their guns. "We'll head out there now."

I described Lana and told them she was very dangerous. They ran out the door, and all of my energy ran out of me. I slumped into a chair.

Lauren made a cold compress and held it to my brow as Betty raided my purse for change and then got me a pop from the vending machine. Inez held my hand as Ava, for reasons unclear, made bandages for each ankle using toilet paper.

Five minutes later, Rex burst through the door and ran to my side before crushing me in a hug.

"Are you alright? Carnack called me!" He held me tight against him.

Kelly came through seconds later with her nursing kit. "The sheriff called and said you'd been injured."

My best friend shoed the girls away and froze, spotting the toilet paper tourniquets on my legs and the bandana around the wrist. She gave the girls a wink. "Nice work!"

I sat there and replayed the events of the day as Rex listened and Kelly patched me up. The girls stared at me, giddy with excitement. I left out the part about them tracking me and stealing and driving my car. There was no point in adding a felony to their records.

Rex kissed me. "I'm calling the state police." He stepped out into the hallway.

"You just can't keep yourself out of trouble," Kelly said with a sigh as she finished bandaging my wrist. "You don't *need* stitches, but I'm giving them to you just because."

She nodded toward the girls. "What are they doing here?"

I looked at four girls, who were fascinated when Kelly produced a needle and surgical thread. After what I'd been through, it didn't bother me too much.

"They were playing in the park outside," I lied. "They saw me run in and followed."

"That's right," Betty said. "What she said."

Kelly squinted at the girls with something that resembled suspicion. "Are your parents picking you up?"

The four girls jumped to their feet. Inez smacked her forehead. "Our parents!" And with that they ran out the door.

"Should I go after them?" Kelly stared at the door as it swung shut.

I shook my head, thinking of the two earrings and two backs I'd planted in Betty's and Inez's shorts pockets, Ava's sweater pocket, and Lauren's backpack. "Nah. They'll be fine." I held up Betty's cell phone and, after hacking past the security code, found the app named *Operation Lost Leader.*

I winced as she stabbed me with the needle a little harder than she needed to.

"I'm sure we can find them if we need them later."

CHAPTER FIFTEEN

Rex returned to say the sheriff and deputy didn't find anyone at the house, but they did find that the kitchen had been lived in. They asked for backup from the Iowa State Police for round-the-clock surveillance. But I knew it would be useless. Lana knew how to spot something like that and wouldn't be back once she did.

My husband took me home, made me my favorite macaroni and cheese…from a box, and put me to bed.

I crashed hard but easily, knowing he was downstairs on lookout and from some excellent pain meds Kelly had slipped me.

I slept for ten hours. Which was unusual for me. Normally after a kidnapping and torture, I merely needed a nap. Maybe I was just getting old.

I opened my eyes to see the sun streaming through the bedroom window and Philby on the pillow next to me. She was glaring as if totally disgusted that I'd slept as long as I had.

"Hey." I reached out to pet the feline fuhrer, who stood up, farted, and walked away. On the pillow was a tiny crushed pair of wings. I didn't want to know how many of the mouse-angels were left. I shoved this thought aside and took a long hot shower.

Ten minutes later, I made my way downstairs, where Rex was on the phone. He quickly ended the call and pulled me into his arms, my head resting against his chest. I closed my eyes. My husband didn't have to say anything. I knew he was worried.

"I'm fine," I said as I pulled away. "She only slapped me." Which was true. Truth be told, I was more worried about what she would've done had I not been able to escape.

"Riley's coming over," Rex said. "I've got a meeting with the Feds. They want to be briefed on Lana."

I nodded and sat down at the dining room table. "Just tell them I was right. That I'd been right all along when I insisted Lana was here."

Rex ran to the kitchen and returned with a box of donuts. Score! I immediately dove into the chocolate chip goodness.

He frowned. "I should stay until Riley gets here."

I shook my head. "No, I'll be alright. I've got Philby."

The cat, upon hearing her name, jumped up on the table and severely considered the donuts. She sniffed delicately at a powdered donut and drew back suddenly, her nose coated in sugar. She sneezed, but when that didn't dislodge the powder, she began spinning in place, as if centrifugal force would help.

"Lick it off," I suggested.

To my surprise, she stopped and did that. A look came over her face like I'd given her several mice tied down so they couldn't escape. She began licking the powdered donut. I let her because those weren't my favorite.

Leonard appeared, and when he saw what Philby was doing, he began to whine. When Philby finished with her first donut, I tossed it to the dog.

Rex gave me a quick kiss and then went to the front door. There was a brief exchange of male voices before Riley came into the room.

"Are you alright?" he asked as he sat down at the table.

"Of course I am," I answered, a little insulted.

Riley ignored the box of donuts. "So it finally happened. You were in the same room as Svetlana Babikova."

I nodded. "I told you she was here."

"You certainly did. I'm sorry I wasn't there with you."

"I'm not sure I would've untied you." I lobbed a chocolate chip at him.

"Did she say anything?"

I relayed the conversation, including the head slap and the girls stealing my van and bugging me.

"Don't tell Rex or the sheriff about the girls."

He crossed his heart—something he'd learned from the Kaitlyns. "I won't. But I think I need to make Betty an intern or something. Do you still have the earrings?"

I shook my head. "No. I got rid of them." And you could bet I wouldn't fall for that again. "You let four Girl Scouts bug you, and where does it end?"

Philby had moved on to her third donut, and I tossed the second to Leonard. Martini was a no-show, but this time of day she was following the sun from window to window for one of her many naps.

"Rex said he's meeting with the FBI." Riley frowned.

"Of course. What's he supposed to do? I'd rather they handled it anyway."

He thought about this and nodded. "I also heard that Hilly has been disappearing. Any thoughts?"

That worried me too. "It's her vacation, so I'm trying hard not to overthink it."

"As much as I hate to admit it, this probably means Hilly may not be the killer," he mused.

I had to admit it, that was a relief. "Ahmed's here. Well, not *here* here. He's at a motel in Des Moines." I filled Riley in on that story.

"Still." My former handler rubbed his chin. "It's strange that they think she's in Bulgaria working."

"Who knows? Old habits die hard. Perhaps she couldn't bring herself to use the word vacation. Or she's planning to go there after here to do a job." With Hilly, anything was possible.

"Don't you think Lana will come after you again?" Riley asked. "She may be involved in all of this. I could take some time off the Zimmer case and shadow you."

"And lose out on that gig?" I arched one eyebrow. "Nah. I'll be fine. I'll carry a gun around or something. You need to figure out what happened to Erskine's crop."

He said nothing and made no move to leave.

"Riley." I sighed. "You don't need to feel guilty about the attack. How could you know she'd pick that time and day to strike? It's really my fault for not telling anyone where I'd gone."

"Maybe *I* should bug you," he suggested.

"Not a chance. But if it makes you feel better, I'll keep my cell close and call you immediately."

"You're telling me to leave?"

"Yup." I stood up and motioned toward the door. "I don't need a babysitter."

Riley took the hint. He knew it was no use arguing with me.

I followed him to the door and, as he walked out, and noticed a certain pink-haired journalist in a car out front. I shut the door and leaned against it. Ugh. I'd rather it was Lana.

How was I going to get rid of that annoying reporter? She certainly wasn't going to give up until she had something Pulitzer worthy. Was my past enough for that?

I'd made the news when the vice president "accidentally outed" me. The whole case had gone to court, and I'd gotten a very nice settlement. Then the VP's assistant took the fall and went to prison. The media lost interest, and I changed my name to Merry Wrath and moved back here.

Was my outing even a story anymore? I doubted it. Maybe I should just tell her who I was and let her realize no one cares. That might work. But there was a problem. Would that get her digging into Hilly's situation? She still worked for the CIA as an assassin (who wasn't an assassin). If Medea found out who Hilly really was, she'd have her Pulitzer Prize-worthy story, and there'd be a huge mess.

Especially if Hilly had killed Anna Beth. Even though an idea was starting to form that it might've been Lana, and even though I'd told Riley I didn't suspect Hilly, a niggling doubt remained.

Philby joined me on the couch. Leonard was curled up in his enormous dog bed, and Martini was asleep on top of him, belly up and arms splayed. Philby climbed up onto my lap and started swatting my face.

She often did that. While I was fairly certain my cat liked me, she also liked annoying me. If I had an injury, she'd poke it. If I was exhausted, she'd sit on my chest until I couldn't breathe.

"What is it?" I asked the cat.

She stopped swatting me, and that's when I noticed she was making that horrible sound she does just before barfing. Before I could do anything, she coughed up a perfect mouse skull onto my chest. Then she jumped down and walked away toward the window to take up her surveillance once more.

It must've been one of the mice from the mobile. Great.

I got up and went to the window to see that Medea was still there, glaring at my house. I got out my cell.

"Hey, hon," Rex answered. "I'm about to go into the meeting with the Feds. Are you okay?"

"Yeah. Riley just left. I have a question on something completely different. How do I make a citizen's arrest?"

"You want to arrest somebody?" my husband asked.

"Medea Jones. She's camped out in front of the house. It's annoying."

"Is she in our yard?"

I sighed. "No, her car is parked on the street. She's giving me the willies. Can you arrest someone for that?"

"You can't arrest her for parking on a public street," Rex soothed. "Although, the city does have statutes on parking. If she's there for more than forty-eight hours or violates a Snow Emergency, then we can ticket her."

I grumbled, looking out at the sunny eighty-degree weather. "What if she's parked on the wrong side of the street?" Because we were on the same block as an elementary school, you could only legally park on one side.

"She's parked on the wrong side?" Rex asked.

"Well, no," I said. "But I could drag her out of the car and park it on the wrong side for her."

"That would be assault and car theft." My husband sighed. "Which means we'd have to arrest you."

"Well that won't work," I grumped.

"Merry, I know that tone in your voice," Rex warned. "Don't do anything—"

I hung up and headed to Medea's car. Cutting Rex off meant I didn't hear his threat. It was a thin argument, but hey, I needed to do something about this cotton-candy-haired menace.

Opening the passenger-side door, I sat down next to a very surprised cub reporter.

"What are you doing?" she snapped.

"Why?" I said easily. "Isn't this what you wanted? You've been stalking me, and here I am."

She gave me a look I couldn't interpret before finally speaking. "Who are you?" she asked.

I could've easily told her. In fact, if she'd done any real research at all, she'd have found someone in this town who knew that I was Senator Mike Czrygy's daughter. And if she knew that, she'd know I was that spy who was "outed." Maybe I should give in and tell her. Give her my story. Take the wind out of her sails.

On the other hand, the majority of Whovians of Who's There didn't really know who I was. Oh sure, some did and many suspected, but it hadn't really come out officially. Iowans weren't star struck people. Celebrities were okay and all that, but we didn't let that disrupt our lives.

I needed make a decision and stick with it. Or I could stall.

"Why are you so obsessed with me?" I asked. "There's been a murder, a teenage druid cult…" I weighed my options on the next bit.

Erskine might not like the publicity, but on the other hand, he had hired Riley, and then it was reported to the police. Better him than me.

"And a very important experimental seed corn crop has vanished into thin air. I'm hardly the big story here."

"I think all of those things are tied to you," the girl said evenly. "You're not who people think you are. And that's my story. All these other things are sidelines."

"Who do you think I am?"

"Do you really want to know?" She glared at me.

"What a strange question," I said. "Of course I really want to know."

She snatched up a stenographer's pad and flipped through the pages. "I have a couple of theories. Let me know which one is right."

Oh, this was going to be fun. Like I'd let her know she was right about anything. If she said grass is green, I'd argue with her.

"You are either an AWOL circus performer or"—she looked at me dramatically—"you're a domestic terrorist."

My head exploded a little. "AWOL circus performer?"

She nodded. "Yes. You ran away from the circus as a child."

I had to know…

"Who runs away from the circus as a child? Isn't it the other way around?"

She gave a snarky grin. "Oh sure…that's what you want me to think!"

"I do?"

"Yes, you do." She grinned triumphantly.

"Okay," I said. "I'll tell you everything if you promise that you'll leave me alone."

Medea's hands trembled with excitement as she held on to her pen. "Really? Shoot!"

"You were right. I was born to two circus performers, the bearded lady and the lion tamer."

Medea scribbled furiously.

I was just getting started. "For years I worked as a juggler. I was juggling chainsaws while still in diapers." I hoped she wouldn't ask me to demonstrate. Rex had banned me from garden implements, saying I was a danger to myself and others.

"After a while I started doing the tightrope while juggling chainsaws." I gave a little hitch in my throat. "Until that horrible day when I dropped one of them. It cut the tightrope, and the chainsaw and I crashed to the net below."

The girl's eyes grew wide. Was she salivating?

"The saw cut through the net and hit one of the spotters below." I wiped away an imaginary tear. "Poor Franz! He never saw it coming!"

"You killed him!" Medea announced triumphantly. "So you ran away here!"

Her smugness was almost too much to bear.

I shook my head. "No, I didn't kill him. In fact, it gave him a new job. He's now known as Chainsaw Charlie, the man with a chainsaw embedded in his skull!"

"I thought you said his name was Franz!"

"It was. But Chainsaw Charlie has a nice ring to it, doesn't it? He adopted that as his new stage name."

She scribbled for a moment. "So, you're on the lam, then!"

I leaned forward with a finger to my lips. "Actually, I'm in Witness Protection. Turned out Chainsaw Charlie and my parents were in with the mafia. I testified against them and now am in hiding here." I smiled sympathetically. "So, I'm afraid you can't use any of this because you'll put my life in danger."

I let that sink in for a moment.

"You're joking," she said, defeated.

Yes, of course I was.

"Nope," I replied. "I guess you'll just have to find another story."

"Who's that woman across the street, then?" She pointed at my old house.

"My FBI handler. She visits on occasion to make sure I'm okay."

"And the cop you live with?"

"It's a sham. A cover story."

Medea hung her head. I almost felt sorry for her. "I really thought I had something."

"You could always uncover one of the many meth labs in Bladdersly," I suggested as I got out of the car.

With a nod, I closed the door and walked back into my house. That was one problem taken care of.

To be perfectly honest, there really was a Chainsaw Charlie. I met him in Warsaw. He wasn't a circus performer, but he did have a small chainsaw embedded in his skull. He made six figures on the Polish lecture circuit.

I watched as Medea drove away. I felt a tiny bit bad, but she was young and would find another story soon enough.

CHAPTER SIXTEEN

———

My cell buzzed.

"Hey, Soo Jin!" I said brightly, feeling much better. It's amazing what a crazy lie can do for your spirits.

"Hi, Merry! Can you stop by? Eddie has those results for you."

I heard a man's voice mumbling in the background, and Soo Jin giggled adorably.

"On my way."

I drove over there like the good circus freak I was.

"Come on in!" Soo Jin beckoned me into her office. Officer Ruiz gave me a friendly grin.

"Hi, Eddie," I said. "You've got something for me?"

We sat down in the medical examiner's office. Ruiz was wearing his State Police uniform. I hoped he didn't think this was official business. I really could get in trouble for that if he thought the soil sample came from an investigation.

"Yes." He grinned. He really was a very handsome man. With the jarringly beautiful Soo Jin, they made a gorgeous couple. It was so unfair.

"I had a friend who specializes in soil samples at the University of Iowa look at it."

"And?" I asked impatiently.

"It's very odd." Eddie picked up a file off Soo Jin's desk and handed it to me.

I looked it over. "There's nothing in it?" My heart sank. "Is that what this says?"

He shook his head. "No. And yes. It means there wasn't anything in the soil. And by that I mean no traces of corn. For all intents and purposes, this was virgin soil. It had never been planted."

I leaned back, my jaw dropped open. I hadn't seen this coming. "No traces of…you mean…there was no experimental crop?"

Ruiz nodded. "That's what he said."

"Could he be wrong?"

"No. He's the foremost expert on agricultural soil in the world."

I looked at Soo Jin. "That's a thing?"

She nodded.

The wheels began to turn in my head. "So there was no experimental crop?"

Eddie shook his head. "What it means is that nothing has ever been planted in this soil. There should be spores from corn or soybeans or even weeds. But it's clean. It's never been used."

That meant something different. "That could mean that whoever stole the crop stole the soil too!"

The trooper shrugged. "It's possible."

"It has to be true," I thought out loud. "Erskine's been a farmer forever. He's probably second or third generation. His dirt would've been used for decades."

"I'll leave that with you." Eddie got up and kissed Soo Jin on the cheek. "I left Scotty's phone number in there if you need to call him. I've got to go." He smiled at Soo Jin. "See you tonight?"

She nodded and squeezed his hands in hers. Then he walked out.

Back in my car, I read the report over and over. None of the information had changed since I'd read it in the office. Now I was faced with a dilemma. Take this to Riley, who Erskine hired to find his crop. Or take it to Rex, my husband, the town detective, who was also investigating but was also in talks with the FBI.

Riley, on the other hand, was probably sitting in his office.

* * *

"You're joking," Riley said for the tenth time as he stared at the papers.

I had to take it to him because he'd asked me to look into it. And Rex knew that I was helping Riley. But just in case, I made a photocopy on Riley's machine so I could take the same info to Rex after I got done here.

"The professor's number is on the top of the page," I said. "You can call him."

"Does this mean"—Riley leaned back in his chair—"that they stole the soil too?"

I nodded. "That's what I thought. It's a century farm, I'm certain. The dirt would have spores from all kinds of plants."

My former handler pondered this for a moment. "This doesn't make any sense. Who steals the soil along with the plants?"

"The only other possibility is that Erskine has an acreage that has never, ever been planted. Which also doesn't make sense."

Riley sighed. "Actually, I'm glad you're here. Look at this."

He handed me an insurance form.

"Erskine insured the experimental crop for five million dollars? Where did you get this?"

"I did some research."

"You hacked into the company's database, didn't you?"

"It took many tries to find the right one. You wouldn't believe how many insurance companies are out there."

"By obtaining this illegally," I reasoned, "it won't hold up in court."

"I'm not trying to get my client arrested. I just wondered about his motivation."

"You think he never planted the corn, don't you? For five million dollars."

"It might explain the virgin soil," he said. "To throw the insurance company off the trail."

"It proves that he didn't plant it," I said.

He nodded. "Or it proves that something is wrong with his soil. How else to explain that he's never farmed that plot?"

Riley had a point. And that's when it hit me.

"You didn't hack into anything. The insurance company hired you to find out if Erskine is lying before they pay out."

"You have such a suspicious mind, Wrath."

I pressed him. "Am I right?"

"You're right," he agreed.

"Did you accept their offer?"

Riley nodded.

"Wouldn't that be a conflict of interest?"

"I suppose so," he mused. "I didn't sign anything, just promised to look around."

"And if you find proof, Erskine could go to jail for insurance fraud."

His face clouded. "I know. But if he stole the crop and hired me in hopes of making a fool out of me, he's got another think coming."

It was a dilemma. I couldn't really blame Riley. You can't get money out of a convicted felon easily. And he didn't want to look stupid. I got that. But taking both jobs seemed a little…well, shady.

I sighed. "If that's the case, then we can cross that off the list of reasons why Anna Beth Trident was here. If it wasn't agricultural espionage, then we're back at square one. Who murdered her and why?"

"It could be Lana. I still think it could be Hilly. Or maybe she just ran across the path of a serial killer. Who knows?"

I threw up my arms. "This is so frustrating!"

"Does Rex consider you to be a person of interest?"

The idea startled me, even after it had been brought up before. "No. He knows I didn't kill her."

Riley leaned back in his chair. "Does he suspect Hilly?"

"She's on his list. But you know if Hilly is really here on business, the CIA will just come down and clean it all up." I sighed heavily.

He looked out the window. "Well, the CIA will most likely blame Lana, now that we know she's here."

I rubbed my stitches, which probably wasn't a smart move. It would make things so much easier by blaming Lana. I wanted desperately to believe it. But for some reason I couldn't.

Riley's eyes grew large, and he grinned. "You still think it's a possibility that Hilly killed that woman!"

I shook my head unconvincingly. "No, I—"

He jumped to his feet. "Yes, you do! I know that look! You think I might be right."

"I've never thought you might be right about anything." I rolled my eyes.

"I've been right lots of times, and you know it," he crowed. "What about that time in Paraguay?"

I frowned. "When you thought the prime minister was really an imposter? That was too easy. The fake guy had a tattoo of a heart with a pug on it. The real prime minister didn't."

"And I was right in Okinawa when I told you we were looking at the Yakuza for that hit."

"You're joking. Of course the Yakuza did the hit. They left a note that literally said, *Killed by Yakuza*!"

But Riley was on a roll. "And I was right about Hilly planting that bomb she rescued you from."

I slammed my hand down on his desk. "For the last time, she didn't do that!"

Shockwaves of pain reverberated through my stitched wrist. That might not have been the best idea to prove my point.

Riley smiled then looked past me and narrowed his eyes at the window. "Hey, is that Hilly driving by?"

I followed his gaze to see my friend pass the window in her SUV.

"I'm going to follow her." I snatched up my purse.

"Wait!" Riley got up. "We'll take my car. She doesn't know it."

Somehow we managed to scramble into the car without losing her. As we started down the street, using the usual evasive measures, I couldn't help thinking this was a mistake. Hilly was my friend. How would I explain this if she caught us?

"I don't want you having all the fun." Riley grinned as he drove.

"You just want to prove me wrong," I groused.

My former handler continued to flash that cocky smile. "There's that too. But hey, you might get lucky. This might prove me wrong."

I thought about this as we drove through town.

"Let's cast all prejudice aside and consider this logically. You put aside your dislike for Hilly, and I'll put aside my friendship. What do you think?"

Hilly passed the city limit and was heading out of town. Riley pulled in one car behind her. As far as it seemed, she had no idea we were following her. Following someone is not easy, especially in a small town with little traffic. Still, we had this huge red pickup in front of us, which helped. I was just happy we weren't behind a tractor. Those things were aggravatingly slow.

"Okay," Riley reasoned. "Strictly rational. You have to take into account a few things. One, you found her behind that restaurant. If she was looking for you, why was she hiding?"

"To surprise me?" My voice was laden with wishful thinking.

He gave me a look. "Why would she try to surprise you? You barely knew her."

"That's not true," I said before my brain caught up with my mouth—something that happened far too often. "I mean, aside from our first run-in, our paths crossed a couple of times, and we had drinks or coffee."

"A couple of times in all your years of employment. Face it… You know Ahmed more intimately."

I opened my mouth to say something but then closed it. It was true I'd talked to Ahmed more frequently since I started selling cookies. I did have way more contact with him than with Hilly.

"I'll grant you that," was all I said.

"So," he continued, "why would she come here and hide out behind the restaurant you and Rex were in? And why hide out by the dumpster? I have to wonder if she was waiting, trying to get your attention to lure you back there and take you out."

"But"—I held up an index finger—"she didn't take me out."

"Because she knew you were with Rex. Someone would come looking for you in minutes. She's in a small town she's not familiar with. It's best to bide her time."

He didn't wait for me to respond. "Second, a Chinese spy ends up dead in your backyard, a hundred feet from Hilly."

I countered, "Yes, but Anna Beth wasn't murdered in my backyard. She was killed somewhere else and dropped there."

"You said you walked across the street to check on Hilly. Isn't it possible she was watching out for you and faked sleeping? Maybe the body was in the trunk of her car and she was going to bury it in your backyard, but you disturbed her."

My stomach slid to my ankles. "I hadn't thought of that."

Riley's argument for Hilly killing Anna Beth Trident was a solid one. "Maybe she was going to dump Anna Beth at the restaurant. Maybe she had no idea I even lived here." Against my wishes, I was starting to backslide into Riley's logic.

"And thirdly"—Riley held up three fingers—"she always seems to be following you somewhere, right?"

I thought about the trip to the zoo in the middle of the night. She could only find me there if she had been following me. Too bad she hadn't followed me to the field yesterday. That would've saved me some pain.

"Those are all valid points," I grumbled. "My turn. Number one, she's been very genuine and friendly. Even asked me to be her best friend."

"Being best friends doesn't mean she can't kill you," Riley interjected.

I tried to picture Kelly doing that. But even all the times she's wanted to kill me…or had a good reason for killing me…she didn't. Would someone like Hilly, who didn't seem to know what friendship was, think the same? Kelly was a nurse—she saved lives. Hilly kind of went the other way.

"Number two"—I held up two fingers—"killing me would certainly implicate her. Why take the risk?"

"That's a good point," Riley conceded. "But if she knew Lana was here, she might've thought she could take the heat off her. Everyone knows Lana wants you dead."

Hilly turned off the highway onto a gravel road that I knew went nowhere. Riley pulled off the road.

Riley looked into the rearview mirror. "Where does this go?"

"It's a dead end. There's an old quarry out there but nothing else."

"A quarry?" Riley's eyes lit up.

I knew what he was thinking. Quarries were excellent places to hide bodies. Did she have someone in her trunk? Wait…maybe it was Lana! That would solve a problem or two!

"There's an old driveway about twenty yards up the highway. It doesn't go anywhere because the house is long gone. We can hide the car there and go on foot."

Riley did as I asked. We got out of the car, and I led the way back to the gravel road. We went two rows into the corn and followed it as it paralleled the road.

"Why would she be out here?" I whispered. "I only know it's here because I know all the back roads around town. She couldn't possibly know about this place. It isn't even on maps."

"Unless she's been here before." Riley looked mournfully at his very expensive shoes as we tromped across the soil.

"She's good at her job," I mused. "One of the first things she's trained to do is scout out the area she's in."

"How much farther?" Riley asked.

His arms were getting scratched by the raspy leaves. Mine were too, but I hadn't noticed. I was torn between the horror of what we might find and the hope that maybe Hilly had killed Lana. But I wasn't ready to share my theory. Yet.

I pointed ahead. "Not too far. Maybe a quarter of a mile."

We picked our way carefully through the cornfield. I kept chastising myself for giving Hilly the benefit of the doubt. If I had to guess, I'd bet Riley was chastising himself for not having a pair of boots in the car. Oh well. Live and learn.

We fell into a companionable silence that comes from working so long together. I knew Riley well. And while he'd given me reason not to trust him in the past, he was someone I could count on in a pinch.

Could I say the same for Hilly? We really did only see each other a few times on the road. Was that enough for her to want to spend her first ever vacation with me? In the middle of Iowa?

I could be so blind sometimes. Maybe it's because I've been out of the spy biz for so long. Maybe it's because I believed her.

"All of these rational theories aside," I hissed, "she really could be here for the reasons she said."

"Really?" Riley's right eyebrow went up. "If she's just driving around, checking out the scenery, why hasn't she doubled back yet? You can't tell me that seeing an abandoned quarry in Iowa is on her bucket list."

I nodded. I'd been thinking the same thing.

I held out my arm to stop Riley in his tracks. "We should be very close. We will have to tread carefully from here on out to avoid being seen. Follow me and do exactly what I do," I whispered.

We moved slowly, keeping an eye on what was ahead. These rows could turn and open up quickly, and we weren't exactly dressed for a clandestine mission. I was wearing a T-shirt, shorts, and sport sandals, which wasn't too bad. But Riley was in a navy polo shirt, khakis, and dress shoes.

"And starting tonight, throw some trekking clothes into your trunk," I insisted.

I tried to remember what the quarry was like. I hadn't been here in years, but I remembered that it was surrounded by trees and rusted equipment. And it was filled with water. In high school, we used to come here to swim. That is…until they started finding bodies. It turned out that the crime syndicate in Des Moines discovered our watering hole and had been using it as a watery grave.

A couple of kids had been fishing, when one of them reeled in a human leg. We never went swimming there again. The authorities dredged the water and found seven corpses in all. Most of them were wrapped up. Written on one of the corpses in black marker were the words *Richie Did It!* But Richie was never found.

Splash!

The sound of something hitting water close by made me stop in my tracks. Riley nodded, indicating he'd heard it too.

Then an engine started, and we heard the crunch of gravel under tires.

I started running with Riley on my heels. We burst out of the corn at the edge of the quarry just in time to see the rear corner of a black SUV turning into the foliage ahead. I motioned for Riley to stay and ran after it, keeping to the bushes for cover. I made it just in time to see the license plate before it sped off.

It was Hilly's. I was sure of that.

CHAPTER SEVENTEEN

———

"Anything?" Riley asked when I returned.

I doubled over, hands on my knees, panting for breath. "It was her alright."

Riley's eyebrows went up. "Are you sure?"

"Of course I'm sure. I memorized her license plate when she first parked her car in my driveway." Did he really think I'd forget my training?

He reached out and put his hands on my shoulders. "I'm sorry, Wrath. I really wanted to be wrong."

I shrugged him off. "Just because she dumped something doesn't mean it was a body. Maybe it was garbage, or some cumbersome item she picked up somewhere, or some uranium…"

"…or a weapon used to murder Anna Beth. Or another body."

I stared at him. "You still think she might have been here for someone else?"

He shrugged. "I'm saying we have to be open to every possibility."

"It could be Lana," I suggested.

Riley thought about that. "You know what? You may be right. We need to find out who's down there."

I walked over to the edge and looked over. I couldn't see anything. Too bad there wasn't a ledge or something that could snag a body in mid-drop.

Riley pulled out his cell. "We should call Sheriff Carnack. He could bring the manpower to search the water."

I shook my head. "No. I've had enough of this. We're going down there. Now." I needed to know who or what was now sinking into the water below.

This was easier said than done. There wasn't exactly a staircase to conveniently take us to the bottom. The walls were sheer granite.

"Have you done any rock climbing?" Riley folded his arms over his chest. "Because I don't remember you doing that."

I rolled my eyes. "I'm a Girl Scout leader. I can teach ropes course and zip line, and I've climbed the rock wall at camp."

"This is significantly harder than a plastic wall with foot and handholds."

He was right, but I didn't want him to know that.

"Do you have any rope in your car?"

With a heavy sigh, Riley nodded and took off down the drive to the gravel road. It would take him about ten minutes to get to the car and another two to drive back.

I sat down on the edge of the rock, my legs dangling beneath me, and stared at the water, wishing I had X-ray vision. Too bad that wasn't possible. It would've made my life as a spy much easier. I'd have been able to see the .50-caliber gun through the post office walls in Porvoo.

Was I right to do this now? I mean, besides the fact it was incredibly stupid and dangerous—something that had never stopped me before, with mixed results at best. We could call Carnack, and he'd be only too happy to drag the reservoir. But what if it was nothing? Then we'd be wasting his time and taxpayer money.

Riley was right. I hated that. It wasn't his fault, and looking at things dispassionately was the correct course of action. Maybe I was becoming too trusting. That was a dangerous problem for a spy, but in a small town, it was important.

I'd been away from the game for a long time. Long enough to be more civilian than spy. Did Hilly play me?

"Of course she did," I grumbled and threw a rock into the water below. "Hell, *I'd* play me."

Taking advantage of people was the first thing we were trained on. *Trust no one. Always be vigilant.* Those were slogans hammered into my head for years. Too bad they never told us to be wary of assassins (who weren't assassins) who showed up on your doorstep for a vacation and a chance to become BFFs.

Riley's car appeared, and he parked and got out. I joined him at the trunk. When he opened it, I gasped. Now I really knew I was off my instincts.

"Are those," I asked, "Twinkies?"

Riley turned white as a sheet, which, considering his natural golden glow, was saying something. I guess he hadn't thought about the thirty or forty boxes of assorted Hostess products in his trunk.

"And Ding Dongs? Cupcakes?" I opened a box and stuffed an apple fruit pie in my mouth. For energy, of course.

I reached for his head and tugged on his hair. It didn't come off.

"What are you doing?" He slapped my hands away.

"I wanted to see if you were Scooby-Dooing me. The Riley I know wouldn't have this stuff within a ten-mile radius of his precious arteries."

I dug through the boxes and stood up with a start. "Chocolate Twinkies? These are really rare!" I stuffed a few in my pockets.

"This isn't what you think," he said slowly.

"This is exactly what I think." I looked at his waistline. "You haven't gained an ounce since you moved here, and I've never heard of you using the gym. And unless you have a hidden room in your house, I haven't seen so much as a kettle bell. How do you do it? Is it liposuction?"

"This stuff isn't for me," he snapped as he dug underneath the treasure trove of sugary goodness until he brought out a long nylon rope.

"Riiiiiiight."

"Seriously!" He pointed to the trunk. "The boxes aren't even opened!" Riley paused. "At least they weren't until now."

"You tell yourself whatever you need to. I know what I'm seeing." I cried out as I spotted something. "*The Most Stuf*

Oreos! I've never seen these in person, and I'm pretty sure they don't carry them in Iowa!"

It was like finding a talking squirrel or purple swan that belched rainbow glitter! These had a huge thing of filling between the cookies. It was the holy grail of cookies.

"I'm going to have to confiscate these," I said, taking the package and chucking it onto the front seat. I emptied my pockets next to it.

"Hey!" he protested.

"Unless you tell me why you have a trunk full of junk food." By the way, I said this because I knew he'd never tell me without a serious round of torture.

"I don't have to explain anything to you." He sniffed.

"You got any more of those in there?" I asked. But it came out like *mxmphxxch* because I'd manage to stuff two of those enormous Oreos into my mouth at once. I started to choke on the sugary goo, and Riley Heimliched me back to safety as half a cookie shot across the hood of his car.

"Let's just get this over with." He sighed.

I coughed a few times and reluctantly swallowed. "Maybe you're not really Riley! You could be a plant! The CIA has surrounded me with spies for reasons I can't come up with right now."

The sugar pounded through my veins, and it was glorious! I don't know if it was the excitement that we might find Lana dead or the chemically enhanced baked goods, but my head started buzzing.

Riley shook his head. "Here's the rope. How do you want to do this?"

After making Riley swear he wouldn't touch the goods I'd taken from his trunk, I took one end of the rope and tied it around a sturdy tree close to the edge. Too bad I didn't have a harness. That would be the safest way to do it. But I had nylon rope, so that would have to do.

I tied the other end of the rope around my waist and gave Riley a thumbs-up as my sugar buzz sped up, turning my brain fuzzy.

"What's that for?" He frowned.

I rolled my eyes. "In the movies they always give the thumbs-up before going over the edge."

"Name one movie…"

"Just keep an eye on the other end of this rope," I grumbled as I stepped off the rocky ledge and then free fell for about thirty feet, coming to an abrupt halt at the bottom that nearly cut me in half.

I dangled there for a moment, racked with pain and loss of breath. What the hell had happened? The pain sobered me up from my sugar binge immediately as I hung there, spinning slowly.

I'd violated the first rule of Girl Scout safety. I'd been cocky, didn't think it through because of that, and didn't do any safety checks. I just jumped off the ledge and plummeted. I blamed Riley and his trunk full of sugar drugs.

Dangling about five feet above a tiny rocky beach, after I started breathing again, I wiggled out of the rope and shouted for Riley to come down.

"I'm not doing that!" he yelled. "You could've died!"

"But I didn't," I insisted, even though I knew I was going to have a rope-shaped bruise around my waist and would be in agonizing pain for about a week. "Just stay there and keep a look out!"

There was a very narrow edge to the reservoir halfway around it. Stepping up to the water, I stared into its depths. I knew there was a drop just a foot away. This canyon had been dug out straight down.

The good news was that the water was fairly clear. I just had trouble seeing farther than a yard into it. Looking back up at the ledge, I wondered how far Hilly would've tossed the body. You wouldn't want it too close to the edge because that would make it easy to retrieve.

On the other hand, even with her athletic prowess, throwing a body took a lot of effort, more than just dropping it. I had no idea who she'd dropped, but if it was a large person, she couldn't have done more than that.

"What do you see?" Riley shouted down. "Anything?"

"Not yet," I shouted back.

Leaning against the rock wall, I took off my shoes and very carefully stepped into the water. My toes curled over a ledge. When I still couldn't see anything, I backed up, got onto my knees, and leaned forward.

Was that something just beneath me, or was it my shadow? It was a sunny day. I pressed my palms into the water, wrapped my fingers over the ledge, and stared. If only I had superpowers that let me see through things. Wouldn't that be awesome?

Sadly, I didn't.

"Climb back up," Riley said.

Should I quit? Maybe it was time to call the sheriff, even though I wasn't any closer to finding out what had been dropped. What if it wasn't a body? Could it just have been a huge rock? A bag full of clothes? Hopefully it wasn't Wolfie, the red wolf from the zoo. I'd have to kill her for that.

None of this made any sense. Why would Hilly find this place and then come out here to dump something if it wasn't bad?

"Wrath!" Riley shouted. "Come back up here."

I shook my head and stripped down to my bra and underwear. Then I dove into the water. It was lukewarm, which was good, since I hadn't thought about it before diving in. In hindsight, I'd yell at my troop if they did something like this. Of course, that would be after yelling at them for coming down the canyon walls like I did. I was proving to be a bad role model. I'd have to make Riley pinky swear not to tell anyone.

"Merry!" I heard Riley scream as my head broke through the surface of the water.

"I'm fine! I can swim!" I shouted back as I treaded water.

Taking a deep breath, I ducked under the water once more and swam down farther into the reservoir. There wasn't much to see at first. The water was remarkably clear, but the farther down the darker it got.

A few fish darted in front of me, and I jumped. Then I went back up for more air. I may be a strong swimmer, but I couldn't hold my breath very long. One more gulp, and this time I pushed myself hard to swim farther.

Something ahead of me gave me pause. It looked like a ghost with a rope tied around its leg, anchoring to something farther below. I swam over and discovered it was a body wrapped in bedsheets. I couldn't tell if it was male or female. At least it didn't say *Richie Did It* anywhere that I could see.

Up for air once more, I squinted up at Riley and told him I'd found a body. But who was it? My heart beat a little faster in hopes it might be Lana.

"Get out of there," he yelled. "I'm calling Sheriff Carnack."

I ignored him and swam back to the body underwater. Tugging on the sheet didn't help, so I reached for what I hoped was the ankle. Well, it seemed like the ankle, even though it was well-wrapped. The knot was something I'd never seen before, and that's saying something from a Girl Scout leader. Obviously Hilly didn't show the girls all of her knots at the meeting.

Four times up to the surface and back down and I didn't unravel it a single centimeter. I was coming back up for air, thinking I'd swim down to find what was anchoring it, when I noticed the shadows of three people standing on the tiny shore.

"Mrs. Ferguson?" Sheriff Carnack held out a towel, which I accepted since, you know, I was in my undies and all.

The other two men, who were wearing swim gear and diving masks, politely looked away.

After wrapping the towel around me, I asked, "How did you all get down here so quickly?"

Carnack pointed at three rope ladders on the canyon wall. Well, that would certainly make it easier to get back up.

I pointed out the location. "It's about ten feet toward the center and maybe six feet straight down." The divers got into the water and disappeared.

"I have to ask, Merry," the large sheriff said. "How did you know there was a body in there?"

I tried to think of what to say before deciding to deflect. "Didn't Riley tell you?"

He shook his head. "All he said was you guys were out hiking and heard a splash. Although I don't know anyone who'd go hiking wearing those shoes he's got on." He squinted up at my former handler. "He also said you dove in from up there."

And that's when I noticed that the rope was gone. Why had he pulled up the rope? Maybe he didn't want them to know how stupid I'd been, or maybe he didn't want the sheriff to see his trunk full of Twinkies. Were they stolen? Were they *hot* Twinkies?

Focus, Merry! That would be a question for another time.

"Yup," I lied. "That's right."

"That's a fair fall." Carnack tried to hide a grin. "You'd have to be an amazing diver to accomplish that."

"I cannonballed it," I lied. To be honest, I was pretty sure no one would survive doing that, but it would've made me a legend in Whovian history.

Before he could call me out on that, the two divers emerged, giving their boss the thumbs-up. If only Riley was down here so I could point that out.

"Looks like you're right." Carnack nodded at the men.

It took about five minutes to bring the body up. A piece of cut rope dangled from the ankle. Oh sure, it's easy to cut a rope. They hadn't even tried to untie it. They must've been former Boy Scouts, because no self-respecting Girl Scout would use such a cheap shortcut.

There wasn't any room to lay out the corpse. The tiny ledge wasn't big enough for all four of us. I climbed back into my clothes and started up one of the ladders, while the men managed to lash the corpse to a rope and climb up with it.

Back on top, I looked at Riley, who shrugged.

"What happened to the rope?" I hissed.

He gave me a look of total innocence. "What rope?"

"The one in your trunk!"

"There's nothing in my trunk." He narrowed his eyes in a warning.

"Fine," I snapped. "But I still get those Oreos and the other stuff I put on your seat."

For being a large man, Sheriff Carnack had no problem getting up the ladders. He helped the two other men bring up the body. They laid it out on the ground at my feet.

"It wasn't heavy," one of the divers said. "I think it's a woman."

I was having trouble breathing. Mainly because I was about to have proof that my new best friend really was here to kill someone. But who could it be? Was it someone I knew? Was it Lana? If so, I would be grateful for that. I'd pretend to be sad though.

"Remove the sheets please, Deputy Deputy," Carnack said.

"Deputy Deputy?" I asked. I'd never really tried to get to know any of his guys.

He nodded. "His last name is Deputy."

Deputy nodded. "Like Major Major Major Major in *Catch 22*."

"He doesn't ever want to be promoted," the sheriff added. "Although I think Sheriff Deputy has a nice ring to it."

My attention was turned to the body as the men began unravelling the corpse. The body was face up, staring at us sightlessly.

"What?" I shouted. "How?"

This victim did not die of drowning or anything else. This victim died of a stab wound to the back. I knew this because the woman on the ground was Anna Beth Trident.

CHAPTER EIGHTEEN

"Do you know her?" Carnack looked at me curiously.

Riley just stared at her, jaw clenched.

"Yes." I sighed. "That body is the same body they found in my backyard the other day. That's Anna Beth Trident."

"Why isn't she in the morgue?" Deputy Deputy asked.

"She should be…" My voice trailed off.

Sheriff Carnack tapped out a number on his cell and waited. After two seconds, I could hear the bright, cheerful voice of Dr. Soo Jin Body on the other line.

He explained the situation and then waited. I got down on my knees for a closer look. Riley joined me.

"This doesn't make any sense," Riley whispered. "Why steal the body and dump it? She didn't have to do anything—she could have just walked away."

"I don't know," I said slowly. "She's wearing different clothes though. Which is bizarre."

Hilly was odd and had some strange habits, but was stealing a body from the morgue, changing its clothes, and throwing it into a reservoir part of her quirkiness? Or was this new?

Carnack thanked Soo Jin and hung up. "Dr. Body still has Anna Beth Trident in her freezer." He pointed with his phone. "And if this woman looks just like her, then I'm guessing this was a twin."

Riley stood up. "The woman in the morgue is a former spy for the Chinese government. I'm surprised the CIA hasn't claimed her yet."

If Carnack was surprised to hear it, he didn't let on. Deputy Deputy and the other one looked appropriately shocked.

Carnack would have some explaining to do later. He was one of the few who knew about my past.

"Did your research say anything about her having a sister?" I asked.

Riley shook his head. "No. I didn't have enough time to be thorough. But as far as I know, she didn't have any siblings."

I got down on the ground to get a good look at the woman's face. If she'd had plastic surgery to look like ABT, there would be scars on her face, usually near the hairline. I couldn't find any. Not one.

This really was a twin. And worse than that, it looked like Hilly had murdered both of them. Which meant Lana was in the clear. But then, Lana had said there were spies popping up all over the place. How did she know that if she hadn't been involved with or killed Anna Beth?

After a few minutes, the ambulance with Soo Jin pulled up, and she jumped out excitedly and ran to the body. She studied the new corpse with great fascination.

"The other case falls in Who's There's jurisdiction," she said. "But this one falls to County."

Carnack nodded and texted someone I guessed to be my husband. "I'll happily give up jurisdiction to Detective Ferguson." He looked at me and winked. "I don't need the government taking over. It's Rex's headache now."

Rex arrived five minutes later. He gave Riley and me a nod, leading me to believe Carnack's text also included our involvement. As he joined the medical examiner, his eyes opened wide. Either he didn't believe it, or he was seeing that this woman was ABT's twin for the first time.

"Even though it's County," Carnack said, "I'm turning this over to you."

Rex shook the man's hand. "Thanks, Sheriff. Nice to see you again, Deputy Deputy and Deputy Smith."

With that, the three men walked to their vehicles and drove away.

"All right," my husband said with a sigh. "What happened? And more importantly, why aren't you at home in bed?"

I pointed to the car driving away. "How did you know about Deputy Deputy, and why didn't you tell me there was a Deputy Deputy?"

Riley leaned against his car, pretending to be fascinated with his phone.

Rex's right eyebrow went up as he followed my gaze. "This is a thing? Why is this a thing?"

I pouted. "It just seems like you could've told me about that. It's pretty memorable and fun to say."

My husband smiled. "I'm sorry I didn't tell you about Deputy Deputy. Better?"

I nodded grudgingly.

"Can we get back to my original question?" He motioned for Riley to join us. "What happened? And please, start from the beginning."

Riley threw me under the proverbial bus. I say proverbial because once in Ulaan Baatar, Mongolia, he *literally* threw me under a bus. Granted, it wasn't moving and it was to keep me from being shot at, but still.

My former handler pointed at me. "This was her idea."

I rolled my eyes. "I was at Riley's office, and we saw Hilly drive by. We decided to follow her."

"Really?" Rex appeared to be surprised by this. "Why would you do that? Was she acting suspiciously?"

"Kinda," I mumbled. "I was starting to wonder why she was here." I waved at the reservoir. "I guess we know now."

Rex ran his fingers through his hair. "What do you know? Finish the story, please."

"We tailed her until she turned down this road," I replied. "I knew it was a dead end with a quarry. There's really only one reason that an assassin—"

"Who's not an assassin," Riley added quickly.

I nodded. "—would come here. And that would be to drop a body."

"I thought you said her thing was dumpsters?" Rex asked.

"Well, it is. But sometimes you have to improvise."

"Continue," he said.

I took a deep breath, which caused waves of pain around my midsection. Hopefully Rex didn't notice. "We parked at the end of the road and walked through the corn to get here. When we got close, we heard a loud splash. We broke through just in time to see Hilly drive away."

"And instead of waiting for the sheriff to come and drag the lake, you decided to go down there," Rex mused.

"I grew up swimming here. And I know what I'm doing." I left out the part of me screwing up the rope thing. He didn't need to know that. If he did, he'd probably never let me leave the house again without a responsible adult.

"And you found the body." He snapped his notebook shut and looked over the edge.

"This is so amazing! I've never had anything like this before!" Soo Jin shouted brightly.

It always amazed me that Soo Jin never questioned finding a body in my proximity. I decided a long time ago that it was because she had good manners.

We all stepped closer to the body.

"That's some resemblance!" Soo Jin whistled as she knelt by the body. "I don't see any plastic surgery scars."

"I noticed that too." I joined her. "Do you think she's a twin?"

"I'd say it's a given," the medical examiner agreed. "But we'd have to do some DNA tests to make sure."

Riley and I walked back to the Junk Food Mobile while Rex and Dr. Body looked over the corpse.

"Two Anna Beth Tridents?" I whispered. "I can't get my head around it."

He shook his head. "This is beyond weird. Even for you."

I rolled my eyes. "Well, it wouldn't be the first time. Remember those twins in Sarajevo?"

Riley laughed. "I'd forgotten about them! I guess this isn't that rare."

He was laughing because we'd been doing some recon in Bosnia, and everywhere we went, these two goth twins were there. Twentysomethings with long, straight black hair and pasty complexions (and I was pretty sure they were wearing eyeliner), these two always vanished when we tried to approach them.

We also weren't sure if they were male or female. My money was always on male. Anyway, we never did find out who they were until we were in China a few years later. The two of them were running a dark tourism business, promising trips to North Korea and Chernobyl.

Turned out they'd fancied themselves spies for Lichtenstein, but the government never showed any interest in them. So, they switched jobs. And we found out that one was male, one was female. Their names were Vlad and Edna, and they were from Poughkeepsie.

"What do I do now?" I switched gears. "It's going to be tough to hang out with Hilly now that I've found out the real reason for her visit."

"What do you think that is?" Riley asked.

"Obviously to kill these twins." I reached through the open window and pulled out the package of monster Oreos.

Riley rubbed his chin. "I just can't figure out why we didn't know Anna Beth had a twin. And why wasn't she spotted here? It's a small town. I'd think one of us would've seen her."

I threw my arms up in the air. "We couldn't even spot Lana until it was too late!"

"If the Agency sent Hilly," Riley said, "she's not going to tell us, and they aren't either."

Something occurred to me. "Why haven't they picked up Anna Beth's corpse yet? That's unusual, right? I mean, something goes wrong, and the CIA is usually here in a couple of hours."

"That's a good point," Riley agreed. "Hilly would've called them right after the job."

"Maybe she didn't because I found it too soon."

We thought about that for a moment. Knowing that Hilly was here to work changed the trajectory of my ideas.

"Let's say, for the sake of argument," Riley said slowly, "that you disturbed her in the act of dumping the body…"

I picked up the thread. "She ran and jumped into bed, feigning sleep, leaving Anna Beth in my backyard. Did she do it to make it my problem?"

Riley nodded. "She found out you have a husband who's a cop. She probably worried about him and told the CIA to stay away."

"That does make sense. But why not keep the body in her car? What was she going to do with it?"

Riley put his hand on my arm. "The only reason I can think of is that she was going to implicate you by burying her in your backyard."

That hit me like a punch to the jaw. I did have a garden that I'd never planted anything in. I'd tilled the soil but never bought the plants. That would've been a perfect place to hide a body, knowing that I was unlikely to disturb it until next spring. And even then, it was safe to assume I wouldn't touch it.

I shook my head to clear it. "Okay, let's say that's what she planned to do. It would explain why she didn't use a dumpster. It would tip you and me off if we found a dead spy here in town, disposed of in that way."

"We definitely would've known," Riley said. "Langley sent her here to take out Trident. You caught her messing around with a dumpster where she might have been planning to stash the body. When she realized you lived here, she changed her plan."

I groaned. "How could I be so stupid? Of course that's what happened! It makes sense!"

I hated falling for another agent's tricks. Not because it made me look foolish—I did something at every troop meeting that did that. No, it was because I was gullible enough not to think that a friend and colleague was here to frame me.

"Okay, what do we do now?" I asked.

Riley ran over to Rex and Soo Jin, helping them load the body onto a stretcher. My head was spinning with confusion. I brushed all thoughts out of my mind because I had much bigger problems.

Hilly had totally played me. And for that, I was going to kill her.

CHAPTER NINETEEN

Hilly's SUV wasn't in the driveway when we got back. Had she realized she'd been made and flown the coop? For a moment I thought about going over there, but I needed more time to think.

"If Hilly comes looking for me," I said to Rex, "tell her I'm not feeling well."

My husband nodded. "I will." He took me in his arms, and I collapsed against his chest. "I'm sorry, Merry. I know she was someone you trusted."

"Are you going to arrest her?" I asked.

He pulled away and tipped my chin up. "I have to bring her in. In fact, I'm heading to the station to get a couple more officers to help me."

"She's not at the house," I mumbled. "She's probably gone."

Rex agreed. "I have to try. That's my job. Just go to bed. I'll probably be home in a couple of hours empty-handed."

Leonard, Philby, and Martini followed me upstairs, where I collapsed on my bed without changing. Martini climbed up on my chest and passed out on her back, arms and belly splayed to the ceiling. Leonard dropped into his bed on the floor, but Philby didn't join me.

After calling for a few moments, I noticed where she was. The fat feline fuhrer was in the window staring at my old house, her tail switching madly. I got up and turned out the light, joining her at the dark window seconds later. What was she looking at?

Dusk had descended. I stared at my house, running my eyes over the front yard, the windows, and the side facing the street. Nothing was there. After a few minutes, my eyes adjusted, but I still didn't see anything.

Philby, on the other hand, was still agitated. It was probably another cat or a bird that caught her attention. I gave up and got back into the bed. My heart was racing, but that couldn't be helped.

What was I going to do if Hilly was still here? She, I hoped, had no idea that I was on to her. Should I confront her? Would that lead to a fight? And after these last few years, could I take her?

Hopefully she was long gone and we'd never hear from her again. I closed my eyes and wished it to be true. After about twenty minutes of this, I fell asleep.

* * *

I was up at the crack of dawn the next morning, and the first thing I did was look across the street to see if Hilly was at my old house. She wasn't. Well, her car wasn't.

"She's not there," Rex whispered in my ear, making me jump.

"How do you know?"

"I went over"—he held up my house key—"and looked for her."

"Okay," I reasoned. "Then we still don't know that she killed those twins."

Rex cleared his throat. "About that… We found something. It doesn't look good."

I stared at him. Did I want to hear this?

"There was a piece of paper under the pillow in the guest room. It had information on Anna Beth Trident and her sister, Annabelle Trident."

"Anna Beth and Annabelle? What's wrong with their parents?"

Rex ignored me. "It looks like she was here all along to take them out." He handed me the folder that I hadn't noticed him carrying.

I didn't want to read it. I really didn't. But I had to know what was going on. There was no other way.

The page had the CIA logo on it, which was really stupid since it implicated the Agency, and it appeared to be a fax. But I didn't care about that at the moment.

Mug shots of what appeared to be the same woman with two different names stared at me. At that point, they'd been alive. The most interesting thing in the file was the fact that for ten years, the Agency thought there was only one woman—Anna Beth. It wasn't until very recently that they realized there was a sister and that she'd been working with Anna Beth.

Some of the stuff I already knew, in that the women worked for the Chinese government, having been turned ten years ago. Before that, they'd both worked in IT at a major tech corporation.

The women started out in corporate espionage but soon leaned toward military espionage. There was no mention as to why the CIA didn't know ABT had a twin sister who worked with her. And at this point, I didn't care. They were both dead, most likely at the hand of the CIA itself, via my BFF, Hilly Vinton.

"It's kind of strange," Rex started. "Soo Jin called. She believes that Annabelle died before Anna Beth. I'm not sure what that means yet."

I handed the page back to Rex. "What are you going to do?"

"I have to call Ted Vandersloot at the CIA and let him know what we know. I'm sure, as usual, they'll send someone to retrieve Hilly and the bodies."

"You're not going after her?" I asked.

"We are still searching for her. She's considered armed and dangerous. We've alerted Sheriff Carnack and the Iowa State Police."

I shook my head. "I'm sure she's long gone to Bulgaria."

"Bulgaria?"

I waved him off. "Figure of speech."

And then I froze. Maybe she was going after Ahmed. Did she know he was here and that he'd told me about her assignment?

Rex smiled wearily. "At any rate, it'll be a lot of paperwork. I've got to go in early and make these calls." He looked like he remembered something and pulled a newspaper from his back pocket. "I thought you'd like to see this."

The headline on the front page of the *Who's There Tribune* read, *Circus Freak Runs Away—Joins Girl Scouts.*

"Medea Jones." I shook my head. "Honestly, you can't tell that girl anything!"

I kissed him. The newspaper was irritating, but I was more distracted by my concern for Ahmed. I mean, he was one of my best cookie customers! Then again, if he was killed, it would most likely null and void his agreements with the other staff over me sending them cases of cookies for favors done.

I changed into shorts, a T-shirt, and a pair of tennis shoes. As I raced out the door, I remembered Riley. This time I wasn't going into danger alone. I picked him up along the way.

* * *

"Who is it?" a falsetto voice asked through the door. "I've got a huge dog in here, and he likes to feed on human flesh!"

"Ahmed!" I shouted. "It's Merry! Let me in!"

The door squeaked open, and Ahmed, dressed completely in drag, stared at us. I didn't have time for pleasantries. I shoved the door open, and Riley and I entered. Riley closed the door behind us and shut the curtains.

Ahmed was wearing a long blonde wig, a tight red dress, fishnet nylons, and pointy flat shoes. The effect might've had a slight chance of being convincing were it not for the thin mustache and scraggly goatee.

"What's this?" I demanded.

"You told me to disguise myself as a woman and to pretend I had a dog."

Well, that was unexpected. "No I didn't! When did I say that?"

"This morning, when you called," Ahmed said.

Riley and I looked at each other.

"Time to go," I said as I shoved the man in a dress back toward the door we'd just come in from.

Ffffft! A bullet tore through the window and curtains, embedding itself in the wall right between us. As we dove toward the floor, three more shots rang out, making a nice, tight grouping where Ahmed, femme fatale, had been standing.

"I didn't call you!" I hissed.

"You didn't?" Ahmed scratched his beard. "You said it was you."

Riley, who was still standing next to the door, pulled out two .45 handguns from his waistband and tossed one to me. I hadn't thought to get guns, and even though I had no idea how he'd gotten his so quickly, I gave a silent thanks for his being prepared.

"Can you see anything?" I asked as I thumbed the safety off.

He got his cell out, held it up to the security eyehole, and took a picture. Riley studied it and shook his head.

"I can make out what looks like a rifle on the roof of the ice cream store across the street," he said. "But the shooter is wearing a black hoodie and sunglasses. It's too far away to even tell if it's a woman."

"Oh," I said. "It's a woman alright." But which one? Lana or Hilly?

Since the gunfire had stopped, I crawled around the bed. There was a door leading to the bathroom at the foot of the bed and a door with similar locks and fish-eye spy hole next to it.

"Two doors?" I asked Ahmed when I crawled back to him.

That was unusual. I hated shootouts in motels for just that reason: once you went in, there was only one way out. This was nice.

"I don't see whoever it is coming this way," Riley said. "But the rifle is gone."

Ahmed began to whimper. "I will never do another favor for you again!"

"Focus!" I snapped. "Where does the other door go?"

He looked confused for a moment but then got the idea. "There's an interior hallway. Goes to the lobby. They have a nice complimentary breakfast there. They even have a waffle maker."

That did sound good. I turned to Riley. "What do you think?"

"We could be surrounded," he said thoughtfully. "But if this is one of our two suspects, my guess is that she is working alone."

I nodded. "You can't see that there's an interior door from the outside. I say we take a chance and go out that way."

Riley nodded before jamming a desk chair up underneath the doorknob.

"I want to change," Ahmed demanded.

"No time!" Still on all fours, we crawled around the bed toward the other door. Riley brought up the rear.

I held my phone up to the peep hole, took a picture, and brought it down to see what was there. A dark, narrow hallway. I couldn't see the end. Why were they always dark hallways? Why not brightly lit hallways? I could've used that about a thousand times in my career.

I shook my head at Riley. He nodded, shoving Ahmed off to the side of the doorway as I reached up and opened the door, quickly dropping to the floor, gun drawn, as I aimed down the hall.

"No shots," I said. "Let's go."

"You know," Riley said, "Rex is going to be pissed that you got yourself into trouble so quickly after the quarry and Lana's torture hideout."

"Lana?" Ahmed squeaked. "Lana Babikova?"

I didn't answer because I was already halfway down the hall. There were four other doors that lined the hallway. We'd have to be quiet. It was possible that Hilly or Lana could've run around to this side and was waiting to ambush us behind any of them.

"Should I keep crawling?" Ahmed whimpered.

I smothered a temptation to answer that sarcastically. Instead I held a finger to my lips as Riley lifted him to his feet.

"Do exactly what we say," he told the quivering CIA analyst who was dressed like a woman.

Ahmed nodded. He'd never really been a field agent. He probably never in a million years thought he'd be in this sort of situation. I couldn't blame him for being upset.

Riley closed the door behind them and shoved Ahmed against the wall, indicating that he shouldn't move or speak. Then he joined me.

"I'll take the end of the hall," he said with a grin. "Isn't this fun?"

"Can't say I missed the opportunity to get shot in a roach motel," I replied. "Go."

Riley took off down the hallway, and I backtracked to Ahmed, keeping my eye on the four doors between us and the way out. My mind reverted to its training, but in the back of my head, I kept going between Lana and Hilly. Which one was it?

They were both about the same size, although Hilly had a more athletic frame. Lana was blonde while Hilly was a brunette, but that could be obscured by an oversize hoodie and sunglasses.

Dammit. Why couldn't this be simpler? I was getting tired of wondering who was going to kill whom. If Hilly really was my friend, it seemed like she should've warned me somehow with: *Oh, by the way, I'm off to kill Ahmed. You don't mind, do you?*

Someone was running toward us, and I shoved Ahmed to a crouching position as I got in front of him. My gun was trained on the darkness, prepared to shoot if a woman in a hoodie showed up.

Riley emerged, jogging toward us, so I trained my gun on anything that might be behind him. He joined us without even panting. I really needed to ask about that trunkful of junk food. I already felt like I'd gained five pounds at the quarry.

"We have a problem," he whispered as he pointed toward the hall's end. "That's the lobby. And right now, there's a dead hippie slumped over the counter with a bullet hole in the middle of his forehead."

"Milton!" Ahmed squeaked. "He was nice. Let me have extra yogurt."

I ignored him. "She's already there. That was fast."

Riley nodded. "Looks like a trap."

I looked around. "We could go back the way we came. Or through one of these doors."

Riley scowled. "I hate getting civilians involved needlessly. Look at poor Milton."

Ahmed groaned. "He loaned me this outfit. I think it was his."

"Right," I said. "Back the way we came."

I opened the door and swept the room. Nothing had changed, but I still checked under the bed, in the closet, and the shower. Then I motioned for Ahmed and Riley to come in.

Riley closed and locked the door behind him, shoving a cheap nightstand against it.

We were officially barricaded in.

Riley called 9-1-1 and requested a SWAT team while I broke the bathroom mirror and used a shard to check the window. I knew where the sniper would've been but couldn't see her.

Riley finished his call and, after shoving Ahmed into the bathtub, joined me.

"They're on their way."

"You know what?" I said. "It's kind of nice to work in a First World country where we can just call for backup."

I wasn't kidding. Most of the time Riley and I had worked in places where we were the only cavalry. Knowing that Des Moines' best was on its way was a small consolation. They'd pull up and surround the hotel, following the standard playbook.

The only problem was they didn't know how a spy sniper would operate. That came down to Riley and me.

"What do you think?" I asked as we stood against the wall between the bathroom and the door to the outside.

Riley shrugged. "I thought I'd miss all this, quite frankly. But right now I wish I was back in my little office in Who's There."

I agreed. "Yeah. I know how you feel. I've been kidnapped twice, tied to a bed and threatened with torture, fell off a cliff, and swam through a reservoir to find a dead body—all in a few days. It's exhausting."

There were no gunshots, no sirens in the distance. It was quiet. From experience, I knew this was misleading. Even if the sirens were closing in, you weren't safe until you were out of the line of fire. And we weren't.

The sound of someone in the hallway running toward us made Riley run to that door and get to the side of it. We couldn't automatically assume it was the sniper. It could've been the maid or the occupants of the other rooms who'd just discovered Milton and were diving for cover.

"Why hasn't she moved in for the kill?" I asked.

"Maybe she decided against it, knowing we are here and armed."

"Ugh." I made a face. "Then we have to explain it all to the local law enforcement. We'll be here hours until they confirm our side of the story."

Riley nodded. "Hilly could now be on her way back to Who's There."

I narrowed my eyes. "Or Lana is halfway into the countryside by now."

Sirens wailed in the far distance. I estimated we had about five minutes.

"You just can't give up the idea that Lana is responsible for this, can you?" Riley shook his head.

"What about you?" I demanded. "I was right. Lana is here, trying to kill me."

We seethed in silence.

"Maybe she's after *you* right now," Ahmed shouted from the bathtub hopefully.

I ignored him. "Well, at least we know it's one of two women."

Riley laughed. "And we aren't any closer to finding out who killed Anna Beth and Annabelle."

"Or who stole Erskine Zimmer's experimental crop," I added. "Although my money's on the twins."

Riley stared off into space wistfully. "I really wanted to solve that one."

The sirens were coming closer.

"Well," I suggested, "whoever comes through that door, we can ask them about it before the shootout." I looked toward the bathroom. "I'm pretty sure you and I will make it, but Ahmed's survival is dicey."

"I heard that!" Ahmed squeaked.

Riley nodded. "I give him 50/50."

I agreed. "Yes, but we're here, which gives him an advantage."

"What if he's right and it's Lana here to kill you?"

I thought about that. "Well then, Ahmed's in the clear. You and I, not so much."

A door slammed in the hallway, followed by screaming and another door slamming.

"She didn't kill whoever that was," I suggested. "But it means she's likely in a room on either side of us."

Riley sighed as the sirens at last hit the parking lot. "So, let's say for the sake of argument that it's Lana. She's probably here to kill you. On the other hand, if it's Hilly, she could be here to kill Ahmed or all of us."

"Hilly Vinton?" Ahmed squeaked, grabbing the shower curtain for support. "You have to get me out of here!"

We ignored him.

"Come out with your hands up!" a man on a megaphone shouted from the parking lot.

"Does he mean us?" Riley asked.

I looked at Ahmed. "We could send him out and see if they shoot him."

"Hey!" Ahmed began to tremble.

Riley shook his head. "He's too unpredictable." He called the police station and was connected to one of the guys in charge outside. "Hey, I'm Riley Andrews," he said. "I'm the one who called you."

Riley explained our situation, and I heard some mumbling on the other end. Then he hung up.

"They want us to wait while they clear the lobby."

"Not a chance," I said. "She'll barrel right through that door."

Ahmed fainted. Which was good because he was safer prone in the bathtub.

An idea occurred to me, and I smiled. "Unless we get to her first."

We left Ahmed in the tub, and after closing the door to the bathroom, we flung open the door to the hall. I took the room on the right, while Riley took the one on the left. We kicked down the doors simultaneously and went in, guns blazing.

I'd always liked that phrase…guns blazing. I had no idea what it means. Who sets a gun on fire? And if you did, it certainly wouldn't operate properly.

The room was empty. I moved quickly to check under the bed and in the closet. The bathroom door was open, and I jumped into the room, but there was no one there. Then I heard it. The back door to the room banged open. She was on the move!

Riley popped in and shook his head, but I was already after the sniper. To my surprise, there was no police presence here, which was bad because they didn't shoot the sniper and good because they didn't shoot me.

The sniper was nowhere to be found.

"Are you sure it was her?" Riley asked as he joined me in the doorway. "It could've been a resident."

I started to move, but something went crunch beneath my feet. Kneeling down, I saw something I didn't expect to see. After pocketing it, I turned to Riley.

"What was that?" he asked.

"An ID card, of sorts," I said grimly.

He narrowed his gaze. "You know who the killer is."

I nodded. "I know who the killer is. I have to get out of here to cut her off at the pass, if she's going where I think she's going."

Riley nodded. "I'll buy you some time. Go."

And so I left.

CHAPTER TWENTY

———

I managed to dodge the police and claim my car without them batting an eyelash. They weren't looking for me. Riley had told them he was holed up with one other guy and a woman. Hopefully the police would see Ahmed in drag and assume he was both.

As I drove out of town on the graveled back roads, back toward Who's There, I knew who I was chasing. The ancient house key I'd found with the initial *H* told me it was Lana and she'd dropped the key to the old Higgins place.

She wasn't after Ahmed. She'd followed me when I took him to the hotel. The phone call about dressing in drag was some kind of twisted joke. Just between you and me, I thought it was a little funny.

After her failed attempt to kill me at the old Higgins place, she'd fled to Des Moines and staked out the hotel, waiting for me to come back. And I'd walked right into it. Sigh. I was definitely getting rusty.

The puzzles of the past week laid out before me as I drove. My former fourth grade teacher, Linda Willard, was a champion puzzle maker and solver. How would she approach the killings of Anna Beth and Annabelle Trident and the crop theft?

I fishtailed through an intersection and slowed down. There was no point killing myself before I got a chance to kill Lana. How did I know where she was going? It was just a hunch, really, but I knew she'd been living somewhere in the area for a while. Somewhere that would be the last place I'd look. Somewhere safe, until I moved in a CIA assassin (okay, we do have assassins, but don't tell anyone).

I'd moved in with Rex before our wedding in January. And since he already had furniture, I didn't need to move anything. Well, that and I knew I could go get anything I wanted by just crossing the street. At the beginning of summer, we started having troop meetings there, but that was easy enough for her to avoid. We never went in the basement. That's where I kept all of my weapons and gadgets, so there was no way they were going down there.

I pulled into my driveway and parked. Hilly's car was once again missing. Across the street was a beat-up pickup truck. That had to be Lana's ride. As I walked up to the door, I noticed it was ajar. I turned and looked across the street, but Rex's car was not in the driveway.

Philby, however, was plastered to the window of our house, meowing animatedly. I couldn't hear it. It looked like the cat had lost her marbles and was yelling at people through the window. Now I understood why she was always staring at my old house with her tail switching violently.

She was warning me that someone else had been in my house. I made a mental note to find what was left of the mobile and give it to her as a reward.

"Merry!" Kelly startled me, and I jumped into a defensive position.

My friend gave me a sarcastic look. "What is going on? I've been trying to call you. I wanted to talk about that job with Riley and…"

I cut her off, quietly explaining what was going on and telling her to call Rex, Riley, and Sheriff Carnack and tell them to come here.

Pulling the .45 from the back of my waistband, I pushed the door open and walked in. There was a lot of activity coming from the basement. I tiptoed across the kitchen floor, dodging all of the creaky boards, and carefully opened the door.

A flash of blonde streaked by below. She didn't see me. My basement was a long room with the stairs at one end. She would be able to see my feet and legs as I came down and would probably shoot at them. I didn't want that to happen because I liked walking upright.

Lying down on the kitchen floor, I hung my head over the stairs and looked around. Lana was in the corner, her back to me, packing up a box. She'd better not be taking some of my gear. I had some real treasures I'd collected over the years that included a hairspray bottle/flamethrower, a mint tin that sprayed knockout gas if you opened it the wrong way, and grenades. Don't ask.

I walked down the steps as quietly as I could, but it wouldn't have mattered if I'd ridden in on a rhinoceros. The woman was screaming at herself and slamming things around. I spotted the package of chloroform wipes. They were a few feet out of my reach. Sneaking up to them, I somehow managed to pull one out without making any noise.

She never knew what hit her.

CHAPTER TWENTY-ONE

———

Rex, Riley, Sheriff Carnack, and Deputy Deputy arrived in my backyard half an hour later, joining Hilly, Kelly, and me. Officer Kevin Dooley and Ahmed inexplicably arrived together, with Ahmed still in drag. I was tempted to take a picture to use as blackmail so I could get out of all that cookie debt, but I was holding on to Lana. I handed over my prisoner, and they took her without comment.

Deputy Deputy and Sheriff Carnack each had hold of one of Lana's arms. The beautiful and treacherous Russian squirmed, straining to get free, while pummeling me with Russian expletives. She really was creative. I'd never heard the one about being half goat, half rat's anus before. Or maybe my Russian was getting a little rusty and she was saying something else.

Rex looked at me expectantly. "Well?"

"Well what?"

"I'm waiting for your monologue."

"I don't monologue."

"Yes, you do. So, get on with it, please," he said with a smile. "Tell us why Lana is here."

Fine. "I don't have any hard evidence, but this is what I'm convinced happened. Lana was here for two reasons. First, to kill Anna Beth Trident. Then, to kill me."

My husband pressed on. "Why kill Trident? Were the Russians and the Chinese working together or at odds with one another?"

I shook my head. "She killed Anna Beth because Anna Beth was really here to kill me. She wasn't after the super seed at all. The fact that they were both in the same place is merely coincidence."

"Oh sure," Kelly said. "It's all about you."

Sheriff Carnack asked, "Why did she dump the body in your backyard?"

I smiled. "She had no choice. Lana had killed Anna Beth somewhere else—my guess is she lured her to the old Higgins place, where she'd been living for months. She brought the body here because she was squatting in my basement. I think she has been for a long time."

"Why move from a hidden spot in the country into town at your house?" Rex asked.

"You'll have to ask her." I pointed at the Russian. "And she won't tell you anything. But I'm guessing that the appearance of ABT meant Lana would have to up her game. It was time to take me out once and for all. And what better place to confront me than my old house? No one, including me, would think to look there. All I'd have to do is walk in, and she'd have me where she wanted me."

Everyone turned to look at the woman, who, under scrutiny, stopped talking.

"I think she was freaked out by me moving Hilly in here that day. She was probably in the process of taking the body out of here when I showed up. So she dumped Anna Beth's remains in this yard and fled. It had the added benefit of implicating Hilly and me."

Kelly mused, "She must've stored her in your freezer chest downstairs."

Wait, what? Now I had to get rid of it! I really liked that freezer—I could fit an entire steer in there! It came with the house!

"The medical examiner's report didn't say anything about her being frozen," Rex said soothingly. "She must have stashed her some other way."

That was a relief. But now I had to bleach my whole basement. Sigh.

Deputy Deputy frowned. "So, I'm guessing she killed Annabelle Trident too?"

I looked directly at Hilly. "No, she didn't. Someone else did that for the same reason, thinking they were killing Anna Beth. But I can't tell you who because I'm pretty sure that's classified."

Rex followed my gaze. He knew what I was saying. He gave me a tiny nod, which told me he wouldn't arrest her until later, and I was going to get pizza for dinner tonight. It's amazing how a couple can communicate.

Kelly interrupted, "So, Hilly killed Annabelle?"

"Of course not! The CIA doesn't have assassins!" I said as I nodded, confusing my real best friend even more. "Here's how I think it went down. Hilly found out about the contract on my life and came here to put a stop to it. Annabelle was here in town, waiting to meet up with her sister.

"But the Agency didn't know Anna Beth had a twin, so the person who killed Annabelle thought she was ABT and took her out. I kind of caught this person in the act. I'd be willing to bet that the first burial place for Annabelle was in the dumpster behind the restaurant that night. The killer then retrieved the body and held on to it until she could dump it in the quarry."

I smiled. "Of course I have no idea who this person was, but I would like to thank them for protecting me."

Hilly scratched her elbow as she stared off into the distance.

I turned on Lana. "And I'd like to thank you too."

Lana started screaming expletives in English this time. One of the men holding her must've increased his grip on her because she yelped in pain.

"You're thanking Lana?" Kelly asked. "Why?"

"Because she killed Anna Beth so Anna Beth wouldn't kill me." I waited a moment for that to sink in. "Not for altruistic reasons, mind you. Lana killed ABT because *she* wanted to be the one who killed me."

Lana glared but said nothing.

Kelly shook her head. "I don't get it. Why didn't the CIA, or anyone else, know Anna Beth had a twin and that the two were working together?"

"It's a good question, and while I don't know for sure, I'd be willing to bet that both women acted as Anna Beth. That way they could spy on more than one person at the same time, and if ABT was targeted, they could both assume Annabelle's identity to get away with it. The CIA eventually figured it out and faxed that info to Hilly, probably after she'd already killed Annabelle."

Hilly mused, "Someone's going to have to do a ton of paperwork back at Langley."

I shook my head. "It won't be me. I nominate Ahmed."

Ahmed said nothing. He and Officer Kevin Dooley were up to their elbows in boxes of peanut butter sandwich cookies.

"So." Hilly cocked her head to one side. "Who stole the farmer's entire crop?"

I was just about to open my mouth when Rex spoke.

"The teen druids."

Every jaw dropped except for mine because I'd already suspected this.

"Kayla and Mike, to be more specific," Rex added. "The others weren't involved."

"I don't understand," Riley said.

"I do." I smiled. "Kayla and Mike wanted to achieve two things—establishing the group as having supernatural powers and to help Stewie."

"Ah!" Riley grinned as he figured it out. "That's why they dumped the virgin soil over the top after they stole the corn! To make it look more surreal."

"Actually," I added, "I think they did that to make it look like aliens took the crops. But I might be wrong about that. I'll put it on the agenda at our next cult meeting." I looked at my husband. "How did you know? I wasn't entirely sure."

Rex nodded. "I found a weird ring in the dirt. It's like a poison ring in that it had a secret compartment that held a note from Mike to Kayla explaining how it was done. We found the now dead plants at a compost plant in Bladdersly."

My jaw dropped. "They *compost* in Bladdersly?"

Carnack shook his head. "It's a front for a meth ring we seem to bust every other month."

"I hope you'll go easy on the kids," I said. To be honest, stealing an entire crop of experimental corn was going to have some harsh penalties. Sown in the spring, the crop would've been nearing its peak. All that time and effort was lost now.

"I'm working with the seed company," Rex said, "to find some appropriate punishment. I don't want those kids to have records. I'm not sure what'll happen, but I've heard they might be detasseling for free next summer."

"That seems fair," I said. It was basically condemning them to three weeks hard labor for no pay, but it wouldn't be on their record, which was something. They weren't bad kids. Just a bit misguided.

"Let me get this straight," Riley said. "Anna Beth wasn't here to steal secrets. She was here to kill you?"

I nodded. "It would've taken her to a new level. She'd never been an assassin before."

"Amateurs." Hilly sniffed. "This is a job for professionals. I hate it when people think that anyone can do my job." It was the closest she'd ever come to defying the CIA rule that we don't have assassins.

Riley asked, "How did Lana find out that there was a contract out on you?"

Hilly rolled her eyes. "We have memos. Duh."

We all turned to stare at her.

"What?" she asked. "I stay connected. A bunch of us have an email loop. I read the memos."

"There are *memos* calling for my assassination?" I asked. I couldn't resist a fist pump. I'd really made the big-time.

"The call for your death died down a bit after you were outed." Hilly nodded. "The hit came from the Chechens, the same ones you escaped when CNN ran the story outing you. You should watch out for them, by the way. As to why did ABT go after that hit? My guess was you were considered an easy one for her first kill. That happens all the time."

Well, that took a little wind out of my sails.

I turned to Lana. "Why did you take so long to kill me? You've been hanging around here for months."

A hostile stream of Russian swearing poured from the blonde like a raging river of fury.

I laughed.

"What did she say?" Rex asked.

"She'd been trying to drive me insane. Lana thought that after a while, I'd be such a fragile mess, she could make it look like suicide."

"Why's that funny?"

I shrugged. "It's hard to drive someone mad when they already are…a bit."

"So, Anna Beth's appearance upped the timeline," Riley mused.

"I think so," I replied. "Lana really wanted me dead, but she didn't want anyone else to do it."

"And here we'd been suspecting Hilly all this time," Riley said.

If Hilly was insulted, she didn't show it. She merely shrugged, probably because she thought that it was a given that an assassin (who wasn't an assassin) would be the first suspect.

"You really are here on vacation," I asked, "aren't you?"

"I was after ABT, like you said. I told the Agency I was going to Bulgaria because I was doing this on my own. So, I came here to see you, claiming vacation. But I have to say, it wasn't a very relaxing one. I guess I thought I'd get more downtime."

"There's never a dull moment with Merry." Rex smiled.

"I think next time," Hilly said, "I'll take one someplace quiet—like New York City."

As Riley and Rex took Lana away to a waiting squad car, I nodded. "Sounds quiet. I do have one question though."

Hilly grinned. "Shoot!"

"It's really none of my business. I mean, it's your vacation, and you certainly didn't have to check in with me. But curiosity is killing me, and I have to know. Where did you disappear to every now and then?"

"Your sisters-in-law's place."

I stared at her. "What? Why?" Maybe she'd been thinking of taking out Ronni!

"Ronni was teaching me how to do taxidermy!" Hilly reached into her bag and held something out. "I got this dung beetle in Des Moines!" She was bursting with pride.

The deceased beetle was wearing a tiny Girl Scout vest with little badges on it. In one hand, the bug had a small box of cookies. In the other, a noose and a piece of paper that said *Knot Tying Proficiency.*

Ahmed blanched.

"I made one for you!" She pulled out another beetle covered in black and white fur. The bug was wearing a mask of Philby's face.

"Thanks!" I took it with delight. "I'll cherish it always." I wasn't sure Philby would feel the same way, but she wasn't getting to this one like she did with the mouse mobile.

CHAPTER TWENTY-TWO

Hilly left the next day, saying before she hit the quiet city of New York, she was first going to head to someplace with a beach. I wanted to drive her to the airport, but she insisted she needed to return her rental car.

I heard a week later that there was a minor skirmish on a beach in Croatia regarding a red wolf that some CIA agent had adopted and taken there without a leash. She sent me a text that read, *Hey! I got a dog!*

The insurance company paid Erskine for the missing crop. They didn't want to, but because "theft by teen druids who wanted to make it look like the work of aliens" was still considered just "theft," they couldn't get out of it. Erskine paid Riley, even though Rex solved the case, because I lied and told the old farmer the private eye solved it.

Rex pulled off a miracle and got the seed company to drop all charges, in return for Kayla and Mike detasseling next summer. They even agreed to a small wage. The two kids weren't happy about it. I took them to Erskine's nonexperimental field and gave them a few lessons. Although that seemed to only terrify them further. I probably shouldn't have shown them the gross fungus they call corn smut. Kayla threw up between the furrows while Mike merely turned an impressive shade of green.

Stewie was depressed that his magical demigod status hadn't made the corn disappear, but he seemed happy that the two cared enough to make him look good. He even offered to help them detassel to pay off their debt. But at 5'1", I knew he was going to struggle with corn that topped almost six feet. I kept that to myself. Maybe he'd undergo a growth spurt.

I attended their next gathering, which took place at dawn in a wooded area about two miles out of town. I drove, kind of suspecting I was only asked because I had a minivan and was able to drive everyone. The ceremony itself was unusual, with half an hour of us painting each other's faces and making bird calls. It wasn't so bad. These kids were kind of nice, once you got to know them.

I'd been thinking of inviting them to come to a Girl Scout meeting, but Lauren and Betty were a little too interested in asking them about human sacrifice, so I put it off, at least until I could come up with a way to discourage that particular interest.

Medea was fired from the *Who's There Tribune* for her harassment against me and for being an all-around pain in the ass to the rest of the staff there. It turned out that Lana was her source for the idea that Anna Beth Trident had been murdered—and she was a good one since she'd been the one to kill her.

Once Medea found out the truth about her source, she asked me if she could join me in the federal Witness Protection program. I said that was impossible (mainly because I wasn't actually in the federal Witness Protection program), but I did recommend she change her hair color, as Lana's cohorts (who didn't really exist) would be looking for pink hair. She dyed it lime green. Subtle.

I heard she got a job the next day with the *Bladdersly Beagle*. That sorry excuse for a paper hired her because they believed she'd uncovered some sort of Who's There scandal and the *Tribune* had hushed it up. I really hoped I'd never see her again.

Lana was sent to a new high-security prison, where she was placed in solitary and monitored 24/7. She'd added an international murder to her already endless list of crimes. The Russians had insisted she'd done nothing wrong, but Hilly dropped me a postcard from the second leg of her trip, saying the Chinese were not happy about the murder of their operative and were currently combing her prison for anyone who'd take the woman out.

My troop was very disappointed that Hilly had to leave. She gave me a box of piano wire and small wooden dowel rods for a craft lesson on making garrotes. Kelly took it from me when I suggested it. Oh well. I'd tell Hilly it was a hit.

As for Riley, I still had no idea why he had a trunkful of Hostess products, and he refused to tell me. I used that to blackmail him into giving Kelly a job as a researcher. He'd loved the idea. So had Kelly, who'd put in her notice the very next day. Riley gave her an insane salary—also as a result the *junk* in his trunk. I'd uncover that secret, but for now, for Kelly's sake, I'd leave it alone.

For his part, Riley had secretly filmed my stupid plummet at the quarry's edge and threatened to send it to Rex. I responded that Rex, knowing that I broke into zoos, fell from trees, and had been kidnapped by a cult of teenagers, would simply roll his eyes. I was sure Riley was saving it until I could steal his phone and delete it.

My new BFF finally made it to NYC. On her last day, she called to thank me for letting her use my house.

"Anytime you want to visit again, just let me know!" I said.

"Thank you! Tell Riley I'm going to make a friend of him yet."

"Good luck," I mumbled.

"Why's that?"

I decided to tell her of my former handler's suspicions. "No matter how many times I tell him he's wrong, he insists that you set the car bomb you rescued me from."

"Oh! He's right! I did," she answered.

"Wait, what?" I was stunned. "You did set the car bomb that almost killed me?"

Riley was right?

"I thought you knew!" Hilly sounded surprised.

"Why would you try to kill me?"

"I wasn't," Hilly said. "I got the cars wrong. You parked in my target's usual parking spot with the same exact black SUV. Sloppy work on my part in not confirming the right vehicle, and I learned a valuable lesson. But hey! You survived!"

"I survived…" I said slowly, "…an assassination attempt for the wrong car?"

She rolled her eyes. "Well duh, but I rescued you, so we're even."

"How can we be even when you're responsible for my almost blowing up?"

"I don't have time to explain. But I do want you to say hi to the girls for me. I'll be sending them some gifts from the road."

That idea had all kinds of horror written all over it.

I heard mumbling in the background.

"Hey! I've got to go. I kind of made friends with a group of Lithuanian supermodels. We're going to see *Phantom*. Bye!"

So Riley was right. Hilly had set the bomb she'd saved me from.

But there was no way that I was ever telling him that…

ABOUT THE AUTHOR

Leslie Langtry is the *USA Today* bestselling author of the *Greatest Hits Mysteries* series, *Sex, Lies, & Family Vacations*, the *Merry Wrath Mysteries*, the *Aloha Lagoon Mysteries*, and several books she hasn't finished yet, because she's very lazy.

Leslie loves puppies and cake (but she will not share her cake with puppies) and thinks praying mantids make everything better. She lives with her family and assorted animals in the Midwest, where she is currently working on her next book and trying to learn to play the ukulele.

To learn more about Leslie, visit her online at:
http://www.leslielangtry.com

Enjoyed this book? Check out these other reads available now from Leslie Langtry:

www.GemmaHallidayPublishing.com

Made in the USA
Monee, IL
03 July 2020